FITCH ON THE ROAD

By

Sheila Brogan

Illustrated by
Howard Gates

This book is a work of fiction. Places, events, and situations in this story are purely fictional. Any resemblance to actual persons, living or dead, is coincidental.

ISBN: 1-4107-7018-4 (e-book)
ISBN: 1-4107-7019-2 (Paperback)

Library of Congress Control Number: 2003095027

This book is printed on acid free paper.

Printed in the United States of America
Bloomington, IN

1stBooks - rev. 10/31/03

Dedication

For Mouse and Biche

Acknowledgment

Special thanks to Carol, Russ, Max and Jessica, for their wonderful help; to Linnie, Kathy and Jackie whose support was always there when it was needed; and to June, for the great idea that was right in front of me.

Our Story Begins ...

Once there was a baby mouse named Fitch. Well, he really wasn't a "baby" any longer, but because he was small, he looked like a baby mouse to most people he encountered. Mice go out on their own at a very young age, and since Fitch's family had been through a bad time with a cat recently, his parents thought it would be best for him to begin to make his way in the world sooner rather than later.

Fitch felt very confident. So he gathered a few of his favorite tail warmers—a mesh one for hot days, a blue flannel one for cool days, a yellow plastic one for rainy days and the green plaid one that he got for his birthday—and packed them into his knapsack. He also packed his *Many Languages Translation Dictionary,* a fresh pair of socks and a piece of good cheddar cheese.

His mother, who was busy with his new sister, Sally, reminded him to take his toothbrush. Then she asked him to take a pencil as well so he could send a postcard home to Strawberry Lane from time to time.

Fitch finished his breakfast quickly because he was getting very excited about his upcoming adventure. He hugged and kissed his brothers and sister good-bye and gave an extra hug to his mother. His father was just leaving for work, so they went down the path together.

"You are an excellent son," said Father Mouse when they reached the fork in the road. "Remember to be kind to all creatures. I know you will have many wonderful adventures." Father Mouse then hugged his son.

Fitch strapped on his Rollerblades, tightened the straps on his knapsack and started off. Skating backward, he waved good-bye to his father until he went over the hill and out of sight. He was on his own with the whole world in front of him.

Chapter 1
Into the Forest

Fitch's father had gone down the path toward the hayfield. Fitch had chosen the fork in the road that went into the forest. The forest held many secrets that he wanted to investigate. The tall pine trees on both sides of the path were full of squirrels and colorful birds that he had never seen before. Violets grew at the base of the large old trees. He thought of his mother and the times he had brought little bouquets home for her. The bright sun was soon up to the tops of the trees, but it was cool and breezy in the forest. His ears perked up and his whiskers twitched; he could hear a brook not far from the path. "What a good idea," he thought. "I'll go swimming!"

He unstrapped his Rollerblades and scampered off toward the sound of bubbling water. At first he practiced his backstroke, then he did a few cannonballs off the rock ledges, and finally he floated on his back staring up into the sky. Mice are natural swimmers, for getting into water frequently allows them to escape from cats. (Cats hate to get wet!)

After his swim and a lunch of cheddar cheese, Fitch felt a brief nap was in order. He began to pack up, rewrapping his cheese in the waxed paper, when suddenly the sunshine was gone! Large angry black clouds began to roll in, and the refreshing breeze now felt cold and sharp. Lightning flashed and cracked across the darkening sky. The low roll of thunder sounded closer every moment.

Fitch quickly gathered up his yellow T-shirt, Rollerblades and knapsack. He had forgotten the first mouse rule: Always know where you can hide. He hurriedly looked around as huge raindrops started to fall on him, and in a minute, he was soaked to his skin. He lifted up several large leathery leaves, but spiders and a small lizard had already taken these dry spaces.

The wind swirled the leaves and rain around Fitch. He began to feel a scary knot forming in his stomach, and he couldn't seem to see any dry safe place to go.

His knapsack and Rollerblades, now soaking wet, were much heavier than earlier in the day. He dragged them along through the mud as he scurried deeper into the forest trying to find a place to hide.

Crack! went a bolt of lightning right over his head. The mouse covered his ears and made himself as small as possible between two

2

huge tree roots, which were next to him. *Crack!* went another bolt of lightning. Overhead a huge branch had been struck by the lightning. Sparks filled the darkness as it snapped off and fell to the ground right over Fitch's head. He curled into a tiny ball and hid in between the tree roots with his eyes squeezed tightly shut just as the branch landed. When he dared to open his eyes and uncurl a little bit, he realized that the raised tree roots had saved him from the huge falling branch. The large pine branch now over his head had made a sort of roof, and he quickly noticed the rain wasn't running down his nose any longer. It was dark in his refuge but since mice can see really well in the dark, Fitch didn't mind. In fact, he began to feel a little happier. He was still soaking wet, but at least he felt safer. His heart wasn't pounding quite as hard and his breathing began to slow at last.

The storm blew ever harder outside all around him, yet he was beginning to feel secure in his new tree-root shelter. "Well, I might as well make myself comfortable," he thought. Fitch began to pull a few pine-needle clusters off the bough that covered his head. The wonderful smell of pine filled the little space between the tree roots. Soon he had a soft pile of fresh green pine needles to nestle down in. He opened his knapsack and took out his blue flannel tail warmer and

3

his yellow T-shirt. He dried himself vigorously with the shirt and put on the warm flannel tail warmer. He could hear his mother's voice in his head saying, "You are such a smart mouse, Fitch. I know you will always be a success."

Soon he felt warm and dry but also a little hungry. "I'll finish my cheese," he said out loud. The sound of his voice startled him a little. The cheese was soft and crumbly, and he ate every bit of it. "Having adventures makes a mouse really hungry," he thought. The rain was still falling, but the noisy storm had rolled away. Fitch curled up in a ball again on his fragrant, soft pine-needle bed. "Having adventures really makes a guy tired," he then thought, and before he could have another thought, he fell asleep.

He awoke with a start. The rain had stopped while he was sleeping, and the moonlight now filtered between the pine branches over his head, casting a pale light into his tree-root nest. Everything was very silent. Then, in the distance, he thought he heard something. The needles on the pine bough over his head trembled in a puff of wind. His whiskers twitched, his black shiny eyes were wide open, but he did not move a single muscle. His whiskers twitched again, and the hair on his ears and neck stood straight up. Then he heard it again.

Whoo, whoo. The sound was getting closer. *Whoo, whoo.* The sound was right over Fitch's head. He froze with fear. He stared up and listened with all his might.

Suddenly, a dark shadow blocked out the moonlight, and his little nest fell into total darkness. *Whoosh, whoosh*—it was the sound of large wings flapping in the silent air. The branches over his head began to sag so low, they almost touched his whiskers. A gigantic owl had landed right on top of him!

Fitch made himself as small as he could. Huge great talons clutched the branches right over his whiskers. The talons slowly stretched open and reclosed, first on the right and then on the left, as the enormous dark shadow shifted its weight from one side of its great body to the other. Fitch squeezed his eyes so tightly closed that he saw stars. "*Whoo, whoo, whoo,*" hooted the enormous shape. *Whoosh!* went the fantastic wings, and then the talons and the shadow disappeared. Fitch's paws were moist with perspiration. Cautiously, he opened his eyes. He could see the moonlight. His whiskers weren't twitching and the fur on his neck wasn't standing up any longer. He felt exhausted. In no time at all, he fell into a deep sleep.

The morning sounds of the forest were all around. Fitch awoke from a wonderful dream of cheese. In his dream, he was just opening a huge round wooden box of a fine aged cheddar, but squabbling crows arguing right over his head made him sit right up. "Silly crows," he thought as he rubbed his eyes and stretched his back paws and tail. "What an exciting adventure I had, and I have only been on my own for one day. Caught in a bad rainstorm, nearly eaten by an owl in the middle of the night; I better not put that in a postcard to my mom," he thought. "She would be frightened to death." He gathered up his things, slicked back his whiskers, wiggled out of the tree branches that had kept him so well protected and started out on his second day of adventure.

The sun was already shining down in warm yellow patches on the forest floor. The puddles left by the rainstorm provided Fitch with a wonderful place to wash his face, brush his teeth and groom his paws and tail. Soon he was on his way down the forest path with the cool earth on his toes and the smell of pine all around him.

As he scurried along, his tummy started to rumble. "Breakfast," thought Fitch. He stopped and stood up on his hind paws; he shielded his eyes with his right paw and carefully surveyed the forest floor.

"Aha," he said, dropping to his scurry position again, and off he went toward a giant pinecone that must have been blown off a tree by the storm. It was so big and so full of seeds that Fitch could hardly drag it behind him. Having learned his lesson about safety yesterday, he wanted to be concealed for his breakfast. Rolling and pushing the cone along the forest floor was such a hard task that he leaned up against it for a moment to catch his breath. "Maybe I'll just eat a few seeds," he thought, "to keep up my strength." The cone was so big that Fitch could not reach between the scales far enough to pull out a seed without wedging the scale up with a twig. When he did that, he was able to pull out a huge soft seed. It was delicious! He gobbled it down. He then pried out another and another. He was starved! With a huge push, the cone rolled under a bush, and Fitch felt he could eat in peace. After he had eaten as many seeds as his tummy could hold, he pried out some extra ones for his knapsack. "It will be a long day," he thought. "It is best to be prepared," he said out loud.

The path seemed to be leading out of the forest. Soon he was out of the cool green pines. Ahead was a meadow filled with tall grass and yellow and white daisies. Fitch scurried along the edge of the path near a ditch. He remembered his grandfather telling him stories about wonderful things you can find in a ditch. Several blue dragonflies buzzed overhead, and he could hear the drone of bees going between the flowers. Suddenly, he stopped and froze in his tracks. Right in front of his nose was a huge red raspberry. In fact, there was a whole bush full of berries—huge, red, ripe raspberries. What a treat!

Fitch started eating them as fast as he could pull them off the bush. Sweet, dark red juice ran down his face and dripped all over his yellow T-shirt. What a feast he had.

By the time he finished eating and found a little puddle in the bottom of the ditch in which to wash his paws and whiskers, the sun was high in the sky. Then down the path he went again until he came to a crossroad. High up above his head was an old wooden marker sign. The print on the three crosspieces was faded, and the wood was gray and cracked. The sign didn't really seem to have any information on it at first. Fitch stared at it a long time, and then the words seemed to slowly appear: ARPIN, 2 MILES, with an arrow pointing to the right; VESPER, 3 MILES, with an arrow pointing to the left; and a cautionary note on the last crosspiece—NEARLY EVERYWHERE ELSE ... A LONG WAY.

Fitch looked around. Everything was quiet. "I wonder which way I should go?" he asked himself. Suddenly several butterflies landed on the ARPIN, 2 MILES sign. As if calling him to follow, the orange and yellow butterflies flew up and circled Fitch for a moment, and then finally they flew off to the right. He grabbed his knapsack, his decision made, and off he went behind them.

Scurrying along the edge of the ditch was easy. Fitch thought about his Rollerblades, but he decided the path was too damp from the rain. To use them, he would have to leave the cover of the

9

overhanging grass and skate near the middle of the path to avoid the stones, and that seemed a little too dangerous after last night.

"Caw, caw, caw." Fitch stood stone still. "Caw, caw," came the call again. Cautiously, he looked up from under the overhanging grass. High over his head were two black crows. "Caw, caw, caw," said the larger of the two as he swooped down and attacked the smaller one. But the smaller one changed direction at the last minute and flew almost straight up into the clear blue sky. The larger crow also made a quick change in direction and shot straight toward the smaller one, who was now cawing with delight from his higher position. With a huge burst of speed, the large crow shot at the smaller laughing one. Suddenly, there was a loud, hard *thump*. Fitch could see that for a moment the two birds had become one large black spot in the sky. There was total silence as the large dark spot became two spots again: one ruffled crow flying slowly to the right and one floppy crow flying to the left. Feathers began to drift down through the quiet air. Just then Fitch thought he heard a tiny voice. He held his breath so he could hear better and squinted his eyes to scan the sky. It seemed to Fitch that something besides feathers was dropping out of the sky. He heard the faint, tiny voice again calling in a language he didn't understand. The small object hit the ground not far from Fitch.

Everything was silent. The silly crows had flown away. Their feathers finished drifting to the ground as Fitch began to relax again. "I wonder what fell out of the sky? I wonder what the little voice was saying? I wonder whose little voice it was?" Fitch cautiously stood up on his hind paws with his hand shielding his eyes from the sun, which was getting lower in the sky now. He scanned the area slowly from one side to the other.

"Au secours," came from the far side of the ditch in the tall grass by the fence. *"Aide-moi, au secours."*

Fitch already had his knapsack off and was digging in it for his *Many Languages Translation Dictionary.* "I've got it," he said out loud as he pulled the dictionary out of his sack. It had a few cheese crumbs stuck to the edge, but Fitch was too busy leafing through the pages to notice. *"Au secours:* French for 'help,'" it said on page 10. He dropped the dictionary back into his knapsack and stood up again, listening and scanning the area near the fence.

His keen eyes noticed the grass jiggle near the base of one of the fence posts. The little voice called out again very faintly, *"Au secours, au ... ,"* and then silence.

"Nothing with a voice that tiny could be a danger to me," thought Fitch as he tucked his knapsack and Rollerblades under some dry leaves at the side of the ditch. He stood up again to get his bearings, and off he scurried toward the fence post with the jiggling grass.

Chapter 2
The Jiggling Boot

Down the side of the ditch Fitch went, through wet sand, around a large puddle, into a bit of mud, which he hadn't noticed, back into the tall grass on the other side of the ditch and up the steep embankment to the edge of the field. Fitch stopped and checked the field from the safety of the ditch. He saw nothing but blue dragonflies playing tag over his head. He saw a craggy rock not far into the field. Scurrying as fast as he could, he climbed up on it, and then, crouching very quietly, he listened. After a moment, he heard a very tiny cough. Fitch cautiously stood up on his hind paws, stretching to make himself as tall as he could so he could see over the sea of tall grass he was in.

The tips of the grass just to his right jiggled again. "Where are you?" called Fitch in his most grown-up voice. "I'll come and help you," he called. But there was only silence in response. Fitch climbed down off the rock and scurried toward the fence post and the jiggling grass. Then he saw the strangest sight. A huge brown leather high-top boot was moving on its own, and he could hear a tiny thumping sound every time it moved. This was what had caused the tall grass all around it to jiggle too. *Thump ... thump ...* Fitch felt he should perhaps be a little more cautious than he had been a few moments ago, so he crouched down behind a rusty tin can to think. Every moment the sun was getting lower in the sky. "I'll have to find a place to spend the night," thought Fitch. Remembering the owl from last night made his whiskers tremble just a little.

"*Au secours,*" said the tiny, faint voice. It sounded to Fitch as if the call came from inside the old leather boot. He was resolved to help! Peeking carefully from behind the rusty tin can, he saw the boot move again. Gathering up all of his courage, he slipped up to the toe of the boot. It had a damp leathery smell and was warm from the sun shining on it all day. Fitch looked around for danger. Everything was quiet. The boot wasn't moving either. Up on the toe of the boot he went, pausing in a crouch for a moment, then he scurried up to the laces. Using the thick old laces like a ladder, he climbed as far up as he could. His sharp eyes peered into the dark inside of the boot. He couldn't see a thing. Maybe he had been wrong about the boot moving. Maybe there wasn't anything inside after all. Maybe it was a

cat trick to catch him. Maybe … Something seemed to roll inside the

boot, and he felt a little *thump* as it hit the side.

"You are in there after all," he said out loud. "I'm going to try

to help you get out," said Fitch. "I think we need to tip this boot over,

but I'm not sure how to do that."

"Au secours," came the tiny voice. *"S'il vous plait."*

"Oh, dear," thought Fitch, "my dictionary is back in the ditch.

Well, I'll just have to solve this problem first because it is too far to go back now." He ran down the laces over the toe and jumped off onto the ground. "Maybe I can push it over," he thought. He leaned against the heel of the boot, pushing with his back as hard as he could. It didn't move. Then he tried pushing with his hind paws, heels dug deeply into the soft ground. He pushed and pushed. The boot didn't budge at all.

He thought about the pinecone. He had used a twig to wedge up the scales to get out the juicy soft seeds. So off he scurried to look for a twig and a small rock. He soon returned with a stone, which was as big a one as he could carry, and after a few minutes, he found a stick. Wedging it under the heel of the boot, he rolled the stone along the edge of the stick to the middle. He was able to lift the stick onto the stone. The tip of the stick stuck up high into the air. He struggled to get on the stone, and carefully, paw over paw, he crawled to the high end of the stick. He was crouched on the very end of the stick, but nothing happened to the boot. Just as he was getting ready to scurry back down the stick, there was an odd snapping sound. The stick trembled and suddenly snapped off. Fitch was sprawled on the ground next to the now broken stick. He lay in a heap slightly stunned—but more surprised than hurt. He brushed himself off and checked for damage. He discovered only a little rip in his tail warmer.

"That could have been a lot worse," he said to himself. He looked up at the boot. The little thumps had started again, and the boot jiggled a little.

"That's it!" he said out loud. Back to the toe of the boot and up to the laces. The laces were strung taut only about halfway up. The eyelets gave way to little hooks, which went up to the top. Taking the end of one loose lace in his teeth, Fitch used the hooks as another ladder and went nearly to the top before the soft leather started to sway and then to collapse. He looped the lace over one of the top hooks.

Shouting "Hold on," he clutched the lace in both paws and threw himself out over the edge of the boot top. He kicked out with his hind paws and tail to give himself as much momentum as possible. He could feel the rush of air over his ears as he swung out over the tall grass. But soon he was traveling back toward the boot. He curled his hind paws tightly in toward his body as he arrived back at the boot, then he kicked them out, pushing hard against the boot. Thrusting his tail and hind paws as hard as he could toward the sky, he swung out again high over the grass. He heard another little *thump* from inside the boot, and just when he thought this plan wasn't going to work either, the boot began to tip. Fitch was hanging on for dear life as the boot fell over in slow motion. He felt himself drop into the tall grass, and before he could brace himself, he landed on the ground with a thud. The top of the boot, which was now on its side, landed at his feet, and to his great surprise, a tawny brown object rolled out of the boot and stopped right next to him. Fitch stared at the smooth round object, wondering what it might be. Then it moved. First it moved a little to the left, and then it leaned a little to the right.

Fitch's whiskers twitched and the fur on his neck stood up. He wondered if he should run away, but as he was on his back, that wouldn't be easy to do. He decided to just lie very quietly and watch.

Out of one side of the smooth, pale brown shell came two little antennae, then a little protrusion, which soon became a worried little face. The little face looked at Fitch and, before he could say a word, vanished back into the shell.

Fitch blinked in amazement. He got to his feet, brushed the dry grass off himself and slicked his whiskers back. He leaned down and said in the softest voice he could manage, "Don't be afraid. Please come out. I won't hurt you. My name is Fitch. I am a mouse gone out on my own to have adventures." Fitch crouched down very slowly and quietly waited. After a moment, the shell wiggled again. One little antenna appeared, then another. Soon the tiny worried face was looking up at Fitch. *"Bonjour,"* said Fitch—it was the only French word he knew.

The little worried face suddenly broke into a big smile. *"Parlez vous Français?"* said the little voice. *"C'est formidable ça–"*

"No, no, no," said Fitch quickly. "I'm sorry, it's the only word I know."

The little antennae drooped and the smile vanished. "I guess we'll have to speak in English," said the tiny voice. "It's too bad."

"You speak English," said Fitch triumphantly. "What's your name?"

"I'm Homer. I'm a snail who went for a drink of fresh rainwater this morning and almost ended up as a crow's lunch," he answered. The thought of his terrible experience made him tremble, and he vanished back into his shell.

"I can understand," said Fitch to the shell. "I was almost a midnight snack for an owl last night."

Homer's antennae and face reappeared, and he seemed a little less worried. "*Merci beaucoup*—I mean, thank you very much for saving me. I was so afraid. It was so dark. I didn't know where I was."

"You fell out of a crow's beak into an old boot," said Fitch, pointing toward the old leather boot next to them.

As Fitch pointed out the boot to Homer, he noticed something he hadn't seen before because the boot had been blocking it from view. Tacked to the fence post was a faded sign, which he could barely read in the gathering dusk. Fitch stood up and walked a bit closer. "Temenos Inn, Bed-and-Breakfast, First Left," he read out loud.

The sky was filling up with pink and red clouds on the horizon. Fitch knew it would be night very soon. He had not found a place to sleep yet, and he sure was feeling hungry now that he had stopped having an adventure.

"Do you have plans?" he asked Homer. "Is anyone expecting you home?"

"No, no plans," said Homer, and tiny tears leaked out of his blue eyes and ran down his face. "The crow carried me a long way from my family this morning. I am all alone now." He sniffed. Crying always made his nose run.

"That's OK," said Fitch in a comforting voice, and he offered Homer the bottom of his yellow T-shirt to wipe his eyes and nose on. "We can join forces and have adventures together. Two together always have more fun than one alone."

"*Mais oui*—I mean, all right," said Homer, looking a little happier now. "It won't be too much trouble for you?" he inquired.

"Not at all," said Fitch, who was delighted at the thought of a traveling companion.

"I hadn't planned to go out on my own," said Homer. "Snails usually don't travel much. But I guess ..." He paused. "Do you think we might try to find the bed-and-breakfast inn you just read about?"

"I'm not sure what 'Temenos' means," said Fitch. "It might have something to do with cats or owls. I'm not sure it would be safe for us."

Homer's face visibly brightened. "'Temenos' is a Greek word," he said. "It means 'sacred place.' The ancient Greeks called their gardens sacred places." Homer sighed. "I just love a good garden."

Fitch stared at him in amazement. "You speak French, English *and* Greek?"

"Well, yes," Homer answered shyly. "But it is a long story. Do you think we can find the inn?"

"Oh, sure," said Fitch. "I'm pretty good at directions, but I think you need to ride in my pocket, as it is getting late." Fitch scooped Homer gently into the pocket of his yellow T-shirt.

"OK down there?" he asked.

"*Mais oui*," came Homer's little voice.

"Hang on, then," said Fitch as he dropped to a scurry position and made his way back to the ditch.

By the time Fitch found his knapsack, he was starved. He pulled some of the pine seeds out and dropped one in his pocket for Homer. While he gobbled down his seeds, he strapped on his Rollerblades. It was too early for owls and too dark for him to scurry along in the ditch, so he made the brave decision to skate down the middle of the path. The sun had dried out the path, and it would be the fastest way to Temenos Inn.

Knapsack on his back and Homer tucked down safely in his pocket, Fitch stood up as tall as he could to get his bearings, then off he went. In a few moments, he saw a pile of white stones at the top of a tree-lined lane, which went off to the left of the path. Outlined in the deep blue fading light he could see a lovely little cottage. The porch light was on, and it looked to Fitch as if he and Homer would be welcome.

Chapter 3
Temenos Inn

"I probably should close the gate," thought the unicorn as she stirred the cheddar cheese soup on her stove. The lovely smell of fresh chocolate chip cookies and homemade bread filled the kitchen. "I guess there won't be any overnight guests today," she said to herself as she stirred in some extra-sharp cheddar chunks and then took the soup kettle off the stove. She took the last pan of cookies out of the oven and put it on the windowsill to cool. The sun had set and the moon would be rising soon.

"Yes, time to close the gate." She took her Chinese lantern off the shelf by the coatrack in the hall and lit the candle in its base. The square lantern was very old, and the beautiful green metal was worn. The candle flickered at first, but then the flame filled the inside of the lantern with a bright light. The dragons that were cut into the pattern of the metal seemed to come to life on the walls of the hall. Every evening the unicorn would go down the front path with her Chinese dragon lantern, close the picket gate and hang the lantern in the archway of the trellis over the gate. She felt that lost travelers would find their way more easily even if they were not coming to the Temenos Inn.

Fitch, with Homer deep in his pocket, made his way quickly down the path. But now they had a problem. In front of them was a lovely white picket fence and a gate with a rose-covered trellis over it. They could have just gone between the pickets, but a small sign by the side of the gate said: TEMENOS INN: PLEASE RING BELL. On the post supporting the rose-covered trellis was a hook holding an old green bell.

Fitch stared up at the chain that would ring the bell. The chain stopped many feet above his head. It would be very impolite not to announce their arrival. Maybe the inn was full for the night. But how would he ring a bell that was miles above his head? Fitch sat down and took off his Rollerblades. He felt Homer moving around in his pocket, so he set him out on his knapsack. Homer blinked his blue eyes in wonder.

Fitch was tying his sneakers and still not able to decide how to solve his bell problem when he heard a noise and saw a wiggle of

shadows that seemed to be coming down the path toward them.

"Quick, cat, hide!" said Fitch in an excited loud whisper. Homer

vanished into his shell, and as Fitch grabbed the knapsack to pull it

out of sight, Homer rolled off onto the brick path.

Fitch had darted toward the rosebushes, but in the excitement, he had been able to grab only one Rollerblade and his knapsack. In his hurry, he tripped over his untied sneaker laces and fell face-first into the soft wet mud under the roses.

Cautiously, Fitch lifted his face out of the mud and opened one eye. He sniffed the air for the smell of cat. He heard the same noise again—it sounded like *clip-clop*—and cats are much sneakier than that. So he stood up slowly and began to brush himself off as he looked around for Homer. Just then the scary light patterns flashed over him again, and he saw Homer right in the middle of the path. Without any thought for his own safety, Fitch darted out to the middle of the path, grabbed Homer and scurried as fast as he could back under the rosebushes. The sound of *clip-clop, clip-clop* was right next to him now, and the frightening patterns of light covered the path beneath the trellis arch.

Homer and Fitch carefully peeked out from their hiding place and gasped. Standing in the archway under the rose-covered trellis was a beautiful, pure white unicorn. Her golden hooves sparkled in the lantern light as she adjusted the candle and closed the lantern door.

Her tail and mane fluttered a little in the soft evening breeze, but it was her lovely ivory horn, which seemed to softly glow, that made them feel very relaxed. Homer made a little cough. Fitch's whiskers twitched.

The unicorn paused and listened, her ears moved a little, as if trying to scoop up every sound. She turned from adjusting her lantern and began to look intensely down at the path.

Fitch's and Homer's eyes followed her gaze, and there it was, caught on a crack between two bricks: Fitch's other Rollerblade!

The unicorn stepped forward a little, and then Fitch and Homer could see her beautiful green eyes looking right at the spot where they were hiding.

28

"Well, good evening, travelers," said the unicorn in a warm and gentle voice. "Welcome to Temenos Inn."

Homer vanished into his shell for a moment, but the gentleness of the voice reassured him and he soon reappeared. Fitch, brushing himself off and slicking mud off his whiskers, decided it was time to be brave.

He stepped out from the cover of the rosebush and said, "Hello. We—I mean I was afraid you might be … well, you know, a cat. And we were trying to ring your bell, but then Homer fell off."

He stopped and went back under the rosebush for a moment. "This is Homer," he said, holding Homer up into the light.

Homer blinked and tried to smile. "I'm glad you speak English," said Homer. "My Greek isn't very good. Pleased to make your acquaintance." And he bowed his antennae.

"I'm Fitch. I'm a mouse gone out on his own to have adventures," he said, extending his paw toward the unicorn.

The unicorn bowed her head and lightly touched Fitch's paw and Homer's shell with her horn tip. Fitch felt warm inside. There was something familiar and comforting about the unicorn that put him at ease.

"You can call me Uni," said the unicorn with a twinkle in her green eyes. "I've just prepared some supper—you must be hungry after your adventures. Would you like to stay here tonight, or do you have other pressing engagements?"

Fitch could feel his stomach rumbling so loudly that he thought it would scare Homer, but before he could say anything, Homer answered the unicorn's question. "I have had more adventures today than I had ever planned to have in my life. I have a terrible headache and …" His blue eyes filled with tears and his little nose started to run again.

Fitch, who had been trying to still look brave, sat down on his knapsack. "We don't have any plans or engagements," he said politely, "but I'm covered in mud and …"

The unicorn smiled. "Don't worry about a thing. Temenos Inn has everything a weary traveler needs. I am at your service." And with that, she whisked the two adventurers on her back, scooped up the knapsack and Rollerblades with her horn, and before they knew it, Fitch and Homer were in the warm cozy kitchen.

"Homer, I think you need a cold cloth for your headache and some fresh lettuce with diced radish for your supper." As the unicorn spoke, she wiped Homer's shell with a damp towel and then put a few ice chips in another towel for his head. Homer closed his eyes as the headache almost magically started to disappear.

"For you, Fitch, how about a hot soapy tub to soak in while I fix some soup and bread for you? I hope you like sharp cheddar cheese soup." Before he knew what had happened, Fitch was neck-deep in warm soapy water that the unicorn had put in a cereal bowl, which had blue flowers around the edge. Fitch felt his whole body relax. He scrubbed his ears and paws and whiskers until they squeaked.

The unicorn put Fitch's knapsack next to him behind the screen she had made with the toaster. "A mole stayed here last winter," she said, "and he forgot some of his clothes when he left. I washed them, but he never came back. I think they will fit you." She dropped a red plaid shirt and some jeans behind the toaster for Fitch.

Fitch was feeling great, and after his second helping of cheese soup, he felt even better. Homer's headache was gone, and he enjoyed the lettuce and radish salad. Everyone had chocolate chip cookies for dessert.

"I have an old flowerpot that I think you will find very comfortable, Homer," Uni said as she spread a few fresh herbs in the bottom of a small terra-cotta flowerpot. "I thought a little fresh rosemary and lavender would give you nice dreams."

Homer was so tired, he couldn't hold his eyes open another minute. He crawled onto the bed of herbs in the cool damp flowerpot, looked up at the unicorn and smiled. The unicorn put the little flowerpot on the windowsill over the sink so Homer would catch the first rays of the morning sun.

"He had a rough day," said Fitch.

"I would love to hear about your adventures," said Uni. "Will you tell me about them while we sit in the rocking chair?"

The unicorn turned down the lights and lit several more Chinese dragon lanterns that were on the fireplace mantel. The room had a lovely glow. Seating herself in her rocking chair, she asked the mouse if he would like to sit on the padded arm of the rocker.

Fitch found it to be a very comfortable place to sit. In fact, there was plenty of room for him to lie down. Fitch wasn't sure if he should start the story from the time when he left home or from the time he met Homer, and while he closed his eyes to think about it, he fell asleep.

The unicorn smiled. The house was very quiet. Only the faint creak of the rocking chair and the distant chirping of crickets outside could be heard. The moon rose and shone in the window. The unicorn felt very, very happy as she and Fitch rocked in her chair long into the night.

Chapter 4
A Surprise

The large yellow eyes seemed to be following him. He became very, very small in the dark corner of the barn. He could smell the pungent odor of a cat mixed with the smell of fresh hay. He was holding so still, his whiskers didn't even twitch. The yellow eyes blinked as they seemed to stare right at him. The large head slowly turned away. Fitch could see the silhouette of the ears and then the body. The tail swayed slightly as the cat turned and walked out of the barn and into the light.

Honk, honk, honk. Fitch sat straight up. He had just had the worst dream of his life!

Honk, honk, came a truck horn outside.

Fitch flopped back down on his soft bed. It took him a moment to catch his breath and to remember where he was. He had saved an interesting snail, found a wonderful place to stay and met a very unusual unicorn.

He looked around at what was evidently one of the inn's

bedrooms. The sunshine was coming in the window and making a sunny place on the carpet next to his little bed. The walls were papered with cowboys and Indians on a sky blue background, and the curtains were patterned with colorful butterflies and cactuses. It was a cheerful and sunny room. The bed was so comfortable. Fitch snuggled back down and started to fall asleep again.

Honk, honk. The truck's motor revved, and Fitch could hear the gears being shifted as the engine faded away.

Fitch sat up, rubbed his eyes and slid out of the warm quilt onto the carpet. He didn't remember coming up to the bedroom. He just remembered the rocking chair and the unicorn's voice.

The mole's jeans and shirt fit perfectly! He scrambled up onto the window-seat cushion and looked out the window. Surrounding the beautiful garden at the back of the inn was a lovely forest with huge old oak trees and tall pines. The garden had lovely flowers and an area with paths and an unusual trellis. Behind the roses, which were all in bloom, Fitch was sure he spotted a raspberry patch! He suddenly felt as if he had never eaten in his life! He was famished.

Hopping off the window seat, Fitch quickly made up his bed and tidied his belongings. He noticed that his yellow T-shirt and ripped tail warmer were nowhere to be seen. "Oh, well," he said to himself, "they'll turn up." Down the stairs he scampered. The front door was open, and the unicorn was bringing a huge box up the path from the gate. The box was so big, she had it in a wheelbarrow, and it still was almost too heavy for her to manage.

"Let me help," squeaked Fitch as he scurried down the path. The unicorn set the wheelbarrow down and pushed her mane back.

"Good morning," she said. "I hope you slept well."

"I did," Fitch replied, "but I had a bad cat dream just before I woke up. I was glad the truck's horn awakened me."

"I've asked them to honk just once, but you know how excited deliverymen can get. I think they enjoy their work," the unicorn said with a smile. "It must be fun delivering surprises all day. I think if you would allow me to place you on the left side of this box, it would balance the wheelbarrow better." Sure enough, Fitch was able to stabilize the load, and they were soon in the toolshed.

Cardboard was quickly torn off and plastic wrap discarded. Spread out on the floor of the toolshed was a collection of white pieces—some long, some short, some curved bits; lots of screws and nuts; two large gray wheels; and a large package of leather straps with lovely brass rivets and fittings.

Fitch climbed to the top of the pile of cardboard to get a better look. He scratched his head. He had no idea what had been in the box except a lot of odd things. The unicorn smiled quietly and said, "It will be a surprise."

Then she cocked her head toward Fitch. "Homer and I were up very early and had our breakfast, but you must be starving. How about some oatmeal with fresh raspberries?" Fitch grinned from ear to ear. "We were out in the garden before the dew was gone," the unicorn continued, "since Homer loves to get a fresh drink of dew when he can. He seemed a little concerned at first, and after he told me his scary crow story, I could see why! I immediately went to the forest and spoke to the crows and the three owls who live there. I explained that you and Homer were guests at Temenos Inn, and they quite understood. Homer seems much happier now. Let's get some breakfast!" While she explained her forest visit to Fitch, the unicorn had closed the door to the toolshed and had headed to the sunny kitchen with her companion. Once inside, Fitch started to devour his bowl of oatmeal with cream and sugar. It had a large pile of fresh raspberries on the top.

He was so busy eating his breakfast that Fitch never heard the knock at the front door, and he didn't look up until he heard the unicorn say to someone, "Here in the entranceway would be nice."

"Yes, the pale green one will go very nicely with the wall color," he heard her continue.

There was the sound of a drill, some tapping, and then another voice said, "I'll do a test call now if you like."

"Test call?" thought Fitch, and he went back to his breakfast.

Ring, ring. Fitch jumped with surprise. *Ring, ring.* Pushing the last scoop of cereal into his mouth, Fitch couldn't stand the suspense any longer. He hopped off the huge dictionary the unicorn had placed on his chair and scurried to the hallway.

The telephone man was just finishing his paperwork, and the unicorn was thanking him for a fine job. Fitch saw a new pale green telephone on the wall.

"If you have any problems, call the number on the bottom of this sheet," he said as he handed the paperwork to the unicorn.

Fitch was full of questions, but the unicorn winked at him and only said, "It is part of the surprise. Let's go find Homer."

Homer, who had spent the morning in the garden, was ready to come into the cool house and give his report on the condition of the garden to the unicorn. He explained the problems he had found that he felt required her immediate attention: aphids on the climbing roses, thrips on the lavender and a family of grubs who thought they might take up residence in the cabbage's roots.

The unicorn made notes while preparing lunch, and even though Fitch had barely finished breakfast, he joined his two friends in the meal. Then, as the heat of the afternoon made them all sleepy, everyone took a nap—Homer in his terra-cotta flowerpot on the windowsill, Fitch on an old sweater in the rocking chair and Uni outside in the green-and-white-striped hammock tied between two old oak trees.

Fitch and Homer so enjoyed their time at Temenos Inn that they decided to stay on indefinitely. This pleased Uni greatly, for she explained to her guests that the inn didn't have many visitors but that she liked to keep her cottage open as a bed-and-breakfast for the occasional sojourner who might need a resting place. Indeed, no other visitors came to the inn in the weeks that followed, but Uni was never lonely now that she had such good company.

Life among the threesome took on a quiet daily rhythm of gardening, eating and cleaning during the day and stories or music in the evenings.

Homer, who hadn't had many personal adventures to tell about, was nevertheless a very well-read snail, as his family put a high value on good literature and education. So he was frequently called upon at night to recount some Greek myth or one of Aesop's fables. Fitch especially liked these because the mouse in several stories gets to be a hero.

Fitch regularly wrote postcards to his family on Strawberry Lane, and from time to time, he got a letter back. His family was still having problems with cats.

Every evening Uni, as usual, would hang the dragon lantern in the trellis arch, and as the lightning bugs came out and the stories ended, everyone drifted off to their beds.

One night the hooting of an owl from deep in the forest awakened Fitch. He was so startled, he got up to have a cool drink of water and calm his nerves. Hopping up on the window-seat cushion, he looked outside to reassure himself. The garden was very quiet in the moonlight. He could see his T-shirt, several of his tail warmers and some tea towels on the clothesline, but to his total amazement, he also noticed a light on in the toolshed!

By instinct, he crouched down out of sight. Slowly, he peeked up over the edge of the windowsill to get a better look at the shed. Not only was the light on, but someone was also moving around in the workshop because he could see shadows dancing inside. Was someone trying to steal the tools? Fitch watched very carefully as the shadows moved back and forth. He heard a buzzing noise, some clicking and the sound of a small hammer tapping.

"They are trying to steal everything! I must run and tell Uni," Fitch thought. But just as he was going to hop off the window seat, the toolshed door opened. Fitch shrunk back into the shadow of the curtains and carefully peered out. Uni had stepped out of the shed into the moonlight, and someone else had stepped out of the shed too. It wasn't another unicorn—it was a beautiful deer.

The deer seemed to be speaking softly to the unicorn. They both nodded, and then Uni touched the deer's forehead gently with

her horn. The deer inclined her head and vanished into the darkness behind the toolshed. Fitch watched as the unicorn turned out the lights in the shed, closed the door and came toward the house.

Fitch jumped off the window seat so he could get back in bed before Uni entered the house. He didn't want her to think he was trying to spoil her surprise by peeking; but in his haste, he forgot about the half-finished glass of water on the floor. Oops! It spilled out all over the carpet.

42

"Oh, good grief," he whispered out loud. "What can I use to soak up this mess?" He seemed to be scurrying in circles as he heard Uni close the front door and start up the stairs.

Fitch was frantic. He grabbed the mole's shirt from the chair, and just as he dropped it over the spilled water, the night-light in his bedroom clicked on. The unicorn stood in his doorway. "Fitch," she whispered in a soft voice, "is everything all right?"

"All right? Well, yes—I mean, no," Fitch stammered. "I'm sorry, Uni, I think I've ruined the carpet," he said. He could feel a little lump starting to grow in his throat, and it was hard to talk. "I've spilled water all over it."

"A little water on the carpet? We'll just wipe it up, no bother at all. Here, let me help you with that wet shirt. Look, it's almost dried up the water completely." As the unicorn set the glass on the bedside table, Fitch felt the spot where the water had spilled; it was barely damp.

"I'm sorry, Uni. I didn't want you to know I was awake. I didn't want you to think I was spying on you. I—"

"Hush, hush now. Don't you worry about anything. Tomorrow I'll ask the owls to hoot less. I'm sorry they upset you so much. They

43

don't mean any harm, it's just their way." The unicorn hung the plaid shirt on Fitch's chair and tucked the quilt around the mouse. He was already feeling better, and the lump in his throat was gone.

"You will meet my friend La Biche tomorrow. She lives in the forest and has been helping me with the surprise I'm building in the workshop. We've been working every night, and it is finally finished. Tomorrow you will see the surprise. La Biche will be back for breakfast." Uni lightly touched Fitch on his forehead with her horn. In a moment, she shut off the night-light and disappeared across the hall into her bedroom. The house was quiet again.

Fitch felt very relaxed and very, very sleepy. But questions kept popping into his mind: "I never mentioned that the owls had been hooting or that I had seen the deer. How does Uni always know what is troubling me? Why do I always feel better when she touches me with her horn?" Fitch decided to think about these things with his eyes closed. The next thing he knew, he heard Uni calling him for a pancake breakfast. He hoped there would be raspberries, too!

Chapter 5
A Riddle

Scrambling up on his chair bolstered by the huge dictionary, Fitch surveyed the kitchen. No one had noticed his arrival yet because he had scurried in so quietly. Uni was at the stove pouring batter into the frying pan. Her friend, La Biche, was squeezing oranges, and Homer seemed to be busy rearranging the herbs in his flowerpot. The unicorn and the deer were laughing and talking, and the whole kitchen was filled with the smell of warming maple syrup and cooking pancakes.

"Good morning, sleepyhead," said Uni, looking up and winking at Fitch. "Would you like chocolate chips in your pancakes this morning?"

Fitch felt like doing a back flip. "I love chocolate chips even more than raspberries," he squeaked.

The platter of pancakes, which Uni brought to the table, was full of the best treats Fitch had ever seen: acorn-shaped pancakes with toasted acorns for La Biche, leaf-shaped pancakes with fresh herbs for

Homer, blueberry pancakes for Uni herself and wonderful cheese-wedge-shaped pancakes with lots of chocolate chips for Fitch. La Biche served orange juice to everyone.

During breakfast, Fitch and La Biche had time to get to know each other. La Biche lived in a little cottage in the forest behind Temenos Inn. There she grew many rare flowering plants and raised butterflies that were hired for special occasions. La Biche invited both Fitch and Homer to visit her in the forest. She and Homer then discussed her problems with dusty mildew. Homer was able to give her some good advice.

"Are you ready for the surprise?" asked Uni after everyone had finished their breakfast. Fitch squeaked with excitement, and Homer waved his little antennae. "La Biche, will you take Homer and Fitch out on the front porch? I'll bring out the surprise." And then Uni disappeared out the kitchen door and into the toolshed.

Out on the porch, they soon heard the *clip-clop* of the unicorn's hooves on the brick path. What met their eyes was just amazing! The unicorn was pulling a beautiful rickshaw. The two large wheels were not the dull gray Fitch remembered from when he had helped unpack them. Now they were a deep Chinese red with golden designs painted on the rims. The bars, too, were decorated with an intricate Chinese design. The harness and straps, which fit perfectly on the unicorn, were of soft black leather, and the brass rivets and fittings sparkled in the sunshine. The side panels were Chinese red with black and gold dragons.

Fitch was squeaking and jumping up and down. "Can we have a ride?" he pleaded. "Please, Uni, can we have a ride?"

The unicorn smiled and laughed as La Biche picked Fitch and Homer up and put them on the soft black leather seat. It smelled all new and leathery in the morning sun. La Biche adjusted the harness for the unicorn and climbed aboard.

"Why don't we take a quick run over to your cottage?" suggested Uni.

"Great idea," said La Biche. "I might have another surprise for all of us! But before you ask what it is," she said, looking at Homer and Fitch, "I'm not going to tell." She smiled and her eyes twinkled. "But I will give you a hint."

"Oh, yes, a hint, a hint," said Homer and Fitch together.

The unicorn turned the rickshaw toward the rose-covered

trellis arch as La Biche gave Fitch and Homer their hint in the form of

a riddle:

"I creep in the summer,

Spin in the fall,

Sleep in the winter,

Fly in the spring.

Who am I?"

Fitch and Homer looked at each other with puzzled faces.

Homer disappeared into his shell to think, and Fitch looked very

thoughtful as he sat back on the soft leather seat of the rickshaw,

rubbing his chin. He thought hard. He soon recognized that they were

passing the old fence post where he had first found Homer, and he

was certain the old leather boot would still be at its base. He thought

about pointing out the site to Uni and La Biche, but then he decided

that Homer might get upset at the memory. Just at that moment, the

unicorn looked over her shoulder at Fitch, and he was sure she

winked.

The rickshaw turned now and seemed to be going off into a field of yellow and white flowers. Fitch braced himself and grabbed Homer, anticipating the jolt of descending into the ditch, but to his surprise, there was a little bridge spanning the ditch here, and if you looked carefully, you could see the faint outline of a little-used path leading toward a grove of trees. He sat Homer back down as he noticed several blue dragonflies circling around the unicorn. Just then Homer popped out of his shell and Fitch jumped to his feet.

"Butterflies, butterflies," they both said at once, suddenly understanding the riddle.

La Biche laughed. "You are both very clever," she said, "and you are both right."

Fitch could see they were approaching the edge of the grove, and all around the trees were wildflowers swaying in the breeze. Dancing above the flowers were clouds of butterflies of every color. La Biche asked Uni to stop so she could get out and open the black wrought-iron gate to her property. The gate was in the shape of a large butterfly that opened right in the middle. La Biche pushed the wings open and then helped Uni steer the rickshaw up the path.

As they approached La Biche's cottage, Homer told Fitch about an old Native American legend that said if you had a special wish and you whispered it to a butterfly, it would come true, because a butterfly doesn't have a mouth and can tell your wish only to the Great Spirit. Homer's face got sadder and sadder as he told this story to Fitch.

"That's a beautiful legend," said Fitch as he put his paw on Homer's shell and patted it.

Fitch could feel Homer's tiny shell tremble. He bent down and looked at Homer's little blue eyes, which were filled with tears. Before he could call to La Biche and Uni, they were both leaning over the rickshaw's leather seat. Fitch picked up Homer, who sniffed and disappeared into his shell.

In his softest voice, Fitch asked Homer to please tell them why he was so distressed. Homer's sad face reappeared, still sniffling. "It's my family," Homer said in the smallest voice you could imagine. "I want them to know I'm all right. I want to stay with you, Fitch, and I'm so glad you're my friend, but it's my family. I miss them. I wasn't ready to leave." He wiped his eyes and nose on Fitch's sleeve.

"Well," said Fitch, "I think we've come to the perfect place."

"Indeed you have," said La Biche. "I have hundreds of butterflies who would love to help you find your family. Some of them, who come here to eat, might already know them. While you are enjoying some spiced tea or cool lemonade, I'll do some inquiring."

"Can we have our refreshments in the gazebo?" asked the unicorn. "It is such a lovely day and your garden is so beautiful. I'm sure it will cheer Homer right up! Let me help you bring out the tray with the cold drinks."

Uni looked right in Homer's eyes and then touched him gently with her horn. "I know how much you miss your family, Homer," she said, "but everything will be fine. La Biche has a special way with the butterflies, and I know you will get your wish answered."

The gazebo had a wonderful view of the deer's whole garden, and large clouds of butterflies swirled around La Biche as she wandered among the flowers. Uni poured cool drinks for everyone and served sugar cookies, which were fresh and delicious. Homer noticed small clusters of sulfur butterflies flying away in many different directions, and a few groups of white cabbage butterflies circled the gazebo and then instantly disappeared.

La Biche came and sat down at the table with Fitch, Homer and Uni. "I have spoken to them all," she explained, "and they will be looking for your family. Several of them thought they remembered the day you were, well, stolen. I should have more information by tomorrow. It is getting late, and you know most butterflies fly only in the daytime."

"I feel so much better," said Homer with a smile, "just knowing they are trying."

The sun was getting lower in the sky, and the unicorn thought it might be time to return home. The threesome had enjoyed their time with La Biche and her beautiful garden. Fitch had asked a million questions about all the different butterflies. They had all learned how to fold the special origami envelopes that La Biche used to deliver her butterflies for special occasions. Homer also knew how to fold the lovely pink paper into a flower and a bird, so everyone made lots of origami projects.

"I'll wait here," said La Biche, "to get the information for Homer as soon as possible."

Everyone hugged the deer good-bye as the unicorn hooked up the harness on the rickshaw. "Thank you, La Biche," said Uni. "You have helped us have a wonderful day." Fitch and Homer thanked La Biche for all the treats.

La Biche opened the butterfly gate for their departure and then waved them off until they were well down the path and through the field of flowers.

Fitch scrambled up on the armrest and looked back toward La Biche's cottage to wave good-bye to her again. "Oh, Uni, stop, stop, stop!" he squeaked at the top of his voice. He jumped up and down so excitedly that he almost fell off the armrest.

The unicorn stopped immediately and looked back to see what the excitement was all about.

"Look up, Uni," Fitch said as he grabbed Homer off the seat of the rickshaw and held him up in his paw so he could see over the back of the seat.

"Oh, my goodness." The unicorn sighed with delight. Homer's little antennae were waving with joy.

In the sky over La Biche's cottage, hundreds of butterflies of every color in the rainbow had formed the word "Good-bye." La Biche was closing the gate, and Fitch saw her smile and nod her head as he laughed and waved at her one final time.

53

Chapter 6
An Unexpected Reunion

The new pale green telephone at Temenos Inn never stopped ringing! Every mouse, rabbit and hedgehog in the district was dialing 1-800-UNI-RIDE. Word of the rickshaw rides had spread quickly, and as the summer festivals were approaching, everyone wanted to schedule a ride with their friends and family. Weddings, family reunions and rides for out- of-town guests were also filling up the pages of the booking calendar.

Fitch and Uni had set up a good system to schedule all of the rides. Uni answered the phone, and Fitch was stationed with a pencil and an eraser over the pages of the booking calendar. Most riders changed the date and time at least twice before they settled on the final one. Fitch spent as much time scurrying around erasing the dates as he did booking them. They decided to charge by the length of the ride and not by the number of passengers. Uni had gone to a number of popular locations and timed some nice excursions. This allowed her to suggest to a wedding party, for example, that a ride to the old bridge for photos would take half an hour. Or a group of teens from a family reunion might like to go to the park for a swim, and that would take two to three hours. It was interesting to Fitch that most families seemed very happy to have the teenagers gone for several hours, and they really never argued about the price.

Just as the unicorn started to sip her iced tea one Friday afternoon, the telephone rang again. "Uni Rickshaw Rides reservations," she said into the pale green telephone. Her face became puzzled, and Fitch looked up as she started to pace and motion him over to her. She repeated, "Uni Rickshaw Rides, may I help you?" Her brow furrowed as she listened into the receiver for several minutes.

Finally, she was able to get a word in edgewise: "Just a moment, please." Then, covering the mouthpiece, she whispered to Fitch, "Could you take this, please? I'm talking with someone who is speaking Ancient Mouse. My Ancient Mouse is really not very good."

Fitch took the receiver and, smiling, said in his most formal Ancient Mouse, *"E-Reek"* (Ancient Mouse for "hello").

Fitch was delighted to have an opportunity to speak in Ancient Mouse. It had been the language of his ancestors and was rarely heard in the district any longer. Fitch had spent several winters with his grandfather, and on those long nights in the mouse hole, his grandfather had taught him many, many things, like the Ancient Mouse language.

His grandfather had come to the area as a young mouse on a large freight ship. He and his brothers did not enjoy the trip. They had been quite seasick, so once they reached dry land again, each vowed never to leave it. Fitch's grandfather had met Grandmother Mouse in the port, and taking an immediate fancy to each other, they decided to catch the first hay wagon heading west. They soon found themselves in a wonderful warm barn with cows, pigs and lots of grain. Life was good, and before long, Fitch's father was born and soon all his aunts and uncles.

Fitch was one of the first grandchildren, and he and his grandfather formed a very special friendship. Grandfather Mouse taught Fitch how to fish, collect seeds, make milkweed-down blankets, swim and play many games with a string. During their long winter nights together, learning the Ancient Mouse language had been more fun than work. To keep in practice, Fitch always spoke to his grandfather that way. When they traveled to the local sporting events, his grandfather used that language to talk to his friends from long ago, and Fitch would always be able to laugh along with their jokes. This usually surprised the old mice until his grandfather would say, *"Eereek Fitch, ereekie. Fitch oui reek ooee ea reek ioou reek"* (Ancient Mouse for "This is Fitch, my grandson. Fitch knows the old ways and honors our ancient language"). After he explained this, the friends usually gave Fitch a pat on the head, a big smile and some fresh cheese curds. Fitch could always count on his grandfather, and he missed him a lot now that Fitch's family had moved far away from the old farm where his grandparents lived.

"It is Mr. Ashenbrener Sr., the owner of the Three Corners Cheese Factory," Fitch whispered after a while to Uni. "He is inviting you to give rides at the Cheese Festival this weekend."

The unicorn signaled her agreement with a smile and a nod. So Fitch explained all the details to Mr. Ashenbrener Sr. They set up a start time and arranged to have a shaded area for those standing in line to wait for rides. The unicorn also told Fitch to tell Mr. Ashenbrener Sr. that as a favor to her old friend, she would donate all the money from the ticket sales to the Cheese Museum or the Fire Department.

The elderly mouse told Fitch he was delighted and to thank the unicorn.

After he hung up, Fitch worked out several time slots for group rides during the Cheese Festival, and he had saved two or three spots for special guests, which, the unicorn had explained, would be nice to have in case the mayor or the fire marshal happened to come by.

"Uni, you called Mr. Ashenbrener 'an old friend.' I didn't know you knew him," Fitch said with a note of surprise in his voice.

"I have known him since he first opened the cheese factory many years ago. I was able to help him with a small problem regarding some cats," the unicorn confided. "I guess he didn't recognize my voice on the phone, which was why he kept talking in Ancient Mouse. Perhaps old age is having an effect. ..." Uni paused here momentarily, as though recalling some time long past. "Anyway, I have watched him build his cheese business over the years. The factory now produces some of the best-quality cheese in our area. You know, his sons run the factory now. Mr. Ashenbrener Sr. is retired, but I believe he continues to design the cheese boxes as a hobby."

Before she could go on, the phone rang again. "Uni Rickshaw Rides reservations, how can I help you?" said the unicorn. "Oh, it's you, La Biche. How are you? ... Yes, yes. ... Really, when? ... Oh, that's really very special. How soon? Shall we come right away? ... That's really great news. Homer will be thrilled! ... Sure, we'll see you in a few minutes. Bye."

"Have the butterflies brought good news?" asked Fitch with a hopeful look.

"They have indeed! La Biche wants us to come right over. The lead butterflies are back with the news, and there are others still returning who have a letter for him," said the unicorn as she closed the booking calendar and helped Fitch tidy up the desk.

"Let's not take the time to hook up the rickshaw," said Uni.

"Yes, let's just go the back way as fast as we can," squeaked Fitch, jumping up and down with excitement.

They both went to the garden to find Homer. After a look in the rose arbor and another in the vegetable patch, they found him in the shade of the damp unused terra-cotta flowerpots.

"Hello," said Homer, looking up at Fitch on the unicorn's back. "I've been collecting various moss samples to plant in the spaces between the bricks in the new path." He gathered up the little sprigs he had cut off and put them in a small trug. "I think—," he began again, but Fitch couldn't wait a second longer.

"They found your family, Homer," he squeaked. He started jumping up and down again, and in his excitement, he nearly slid off the unicorn's back. "Quick, Homer, the butterflies are back at La Biche's house. Let's go!"

Homer was so surprised and happy, he dropped his trug and moss sprigs. Both Fitch and Uni saw the tears spring to his eyes before he disappeared into his shell. Fitch slid off the unicorn's back and started to wipe Homer's shell with a soft damp cloth he had brought out with him.

"I knew you would want to freshen up," he said to the shell as he wiped some mud off the top of the tawny brown case.

Homer reappeared, and Fitch helped him wipe his eyes and little nose, which always ran when he cried.

"I'm sorry that—," Homer started to say, but Fitch and Uni wouldn't hear of it.

"You're just so excited," said Fitch. "Here, come hop into my pocket." With that, he gently scooped Homer up and put him in the pocket of the mole's plaid shirt.

"So we're off, then?" said Uni.

"We're off," squeaked Fitch.

The path behind the toolshed led past the orchard and into a meadow of white clover. On the other side of the meadow, wildflowers of every color grew in profusion—red poppies, dark yellow coreopsis, white and yellow daisies and waves of blue cornflowers. The bees were working hard, and a steady stream of them flew back and forth to the white bee boxes in the shade of the old oak trees.

"Oops," squeaked Fitch. He was so excited by all the activity, he nearly forgot to hold on tightly. The unicorn had to slow her pace so he could reposition himself on her back.

"Will La Biche bring us some honey in the fall?" asked Fitch.

"She does every year," said the unicorn. "I like to make berry jam, and we exchange."

Fitch began imagining the taste of honey on freshly baked bread. Just as he was starting to think seriously about food, they arrived at La Biche's back garden gate. The unicorn stooped down, and Fitch pulled the little rope to clang her bell.

La Biche was already coming to meet them, with a stream of butterflies darting to and fro over her head. "I have pink lemonade and shortbread cookies prepared in the gazebo," she said, motioning them toward the stone path to the little white building surrounded by butterfly bushes with large purple-flowered clusters.

Fitch took Homer out of his shirt pocket and set him on the table in the gazebo just as four very large monarch butterflies landed near the lemonade. They were carrying a nearly transparent envelope with a very fragile sheet of paper inside. It was all so thin that you could see there was writing on the inside paper.

The beautiful orange and black monarchs guided the envelope to the place on the table right in front of Homer. Everyone thanked them for their help, and La Biche presented them with some special sweetened sugar water, which they loved. Fitch helped Homer open the envelope, and then Homer began to read out loud:

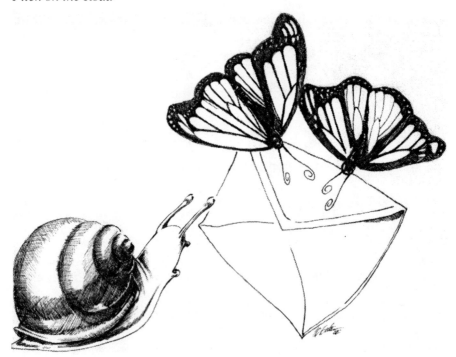

"Our dear son Homer,

You will never know the joy we felt when the butterflies arrived and told us you were safe and well! When your little brother Alvin came home and told us how you had hidden him under a leaf from the crows but then had not managed to escape yourself, well, we were devastated. The butterflies told us all about the unicorn and your friends, Fitch and La Biche. While we miss you very much, we are happy you are making your way in the world. Please keep up your studies and write when you can. We send all our love to you, our

brave little snail son.

Love,

Mom and Dad

P.S. Alvin says hello and he misses you."

Homer sniffed and popped back into his shell. So he wouldn't

feel embarrassed over his emotional state, Fitch cleared his throat and

announced in a rather loud, clear voice that Homer had gone in to

attend to some pressing business. La Biche said she thought they

should have some of her delicious shortbread cookies.

Homer soon reappeared and asked La Biche if there was

anything he might do to thank the butterflies for their help.

"You already have done a great favor for them," she

answered. "The improvements I have made to the flower garden, with

your advice and assistance, have given us many more flowers than we

have ever had. The butterflies all know this, and they are more than

happy to help you. They will be happy to carry messages back and

forth all summer, whenever you wish. For now, though, I have just

told them to return to your family and let them know you loved their

letter."

After everyone finished their cookies and lemonade, La Biche and Uni strolled around in the garden while Fitch and Homer each took a little nap in the shade.

Soon it was time to go home. "I want to polish the brass fittings on the rickshaw so that everything looks nice for the festival," said the unicorn. "And tomorrow will be here very quickly. Would you be agreeable to an early start to the Cheese Festival?" Uni asked La Biche.

"Yes, I love to travel early, before the roads become crowded and the sun is too hot. Shall I meet you at the end of my path?"

"Perfect," replied Uni, bending down to give Fitch easy access to her back. "Give us a call when you are ready in the morning."

The sun was setting as they walked back toward Temenos Inn, and the sky was a deep rosy red.

"Red sky at night, shepherd's delight," said Homer who was riding on the unicorn's horn.

"We should have an exciting day tomorrow," squeaked Fitch, who was already thinking of the cheese curds and dew wine at the festival.

After supper, they all sat on the porch watching the fireflies. As she did every night, the unicorn hung up the dragon lantern on the trellis, and it made wonderful patterns on the path as it swayed gently in the breeze. It had been a delightful day. Homer was the first to say he was ready to go to sleep. Fitch went up to his room too. He had just finished brushing his teeth when he thought he heard a light *tap, tap, tap* on the front door. Then he heard muffled conversation and some laughter. Not one to miss out on any fun, Fitch pulled on his T-shirt and went downstairs to see who had arrived. Perhaps it was La Biche with additional news for Homer.

The unicorn met him at the bottom of the stairs. "Fitch, I was just coming to call you," Uni said with a twinkle in her eye. "There is someone here to see you."

Fitch couldn't imagine who it could be. He scurried the rest of the way down the stairs and into the foyer by the front door. Standing under the light, carrying a small valise and wearing a huge grin, was Grandfather Mouse!

"Reek," squeaked Fitch, and ran straight toward his grandfather with his arms outstretched. Grandfather Mouse bent down and held out his arms to catch his grandson. They hugged for a long

67

time. After a while, his grandfather had to take off his eyeglasses. He pulled out a large red kerchief with a flower pattern on it to wipe his eyes and clean his spectacles.

The unicorn, who had busied herself in the kitchen, now came out and offered some supper to Grandfather Mouse. "Make yourself at home, and when you two are all caught up, I've put an extra bed in Fitch's room for you." Fitch's grandfather bowed to Uni in the manner of the ancient traditions to thank her. "Fitch, help your grandfather find what he needs," she instructed, and touching Fitch on the head gently with her horn, she bid them both good night.

Fitch and his grandfather talked late into the night. Finally, the last words, which could be heard, were spoken as their heads nestled into their pillows. *"Reek reek ree"* (Ancient Mouse for "I love you very much"), said Fitch.

"Reek reek ree," repeated his grandfather.

The air become very still. The fireflies had all gone home to bed. The stars twinkled in the clear night sky, and the unicorn smiled in her sleep.

Chapter 7
The Cheese Festival

It seemed that everything went wrong Saturday morning. Problems had started early at Temenos Inn, and then a telephone call came from La Biche. An order of butterflies for a local wedding had not arrived at their destination. Fortunately, the wedding wasn't scheduled until 1:00 P.M., so she would have time to prepare and send a second order out to them. She would send it by Scurry Express, a local mouse messenger delivery service.

"Unfortunately, this will take some time to arrange, so why don't you just go on ahead without me. I'll be along as soon as I can," said La Biche in a resigned tone.

"Well, I was just going to give you a call," Uni said with a chuckle. "Our day hasn't been much better. Fitch's grandfather arrived late last evening, and although he and I were up early, Fitch was quite a sleepyhead. When he finally got up, he couldn't find his mesh tail warmer, because it was in the clothes hamper," confided the unicorn. "Then, in our hurry to decorate the rickshaw with orange and yellow crepe paper for the parade, everyone got covered in grease from the wheels. We wove the paper in and out of the spokes. It looks very festive, but the grease was ... well, a bit of a problem. Homer, who had gone off to collect some vegetables for the produce contest, discovered that a swarm of angry wasps had taken up residence in the crab apple tree. Grandfather Mouse couldn't find his whisker clippers. ... So you can tell what it's been like around here. And, of course, the phone has been ringing off the hook with last-minute customers for the rickshaw rides." After reciting her list of woes, Uni sighed wearily.

La Biche laughed sympathetically. "I guess my day hasn't been as hectic as I thought! Have you had your breakfast yet?"

"Oh, my, that's another story. Fitch started to—," began the unicorn.

"Never mind," La Biche said gently. "I made sticky buns last night after you went home. I'm nearly finished with the butterflies now. Just relax and get the rickshaw and yourself ready. I'll be over soon with breakfast."

"You're a lifesaver." The unicorn sighed again, this time with relief. "We should be ready when you arrive. Everyone loves your sticky buns."

After cold glasses of milk and La Biche's sticky buns, washcloths were in order for everyone. They were all laughing again, and the mood of the whole company was one of celebration. The rickshaw looked splendid with the crepe paper decorations. All the leather straps were buffed and the brass fittings sparkled. Homer's vegetable contest entries were packed in a cooler. He hoped his novelty carrots in the shape of cheese wedges might take a ribbon. He had also prepared, with Fitch's help, clusters of lavender tied with raffia and small lavender pillows for medicinal uses. These would be sold at the crafts table, and the profits would go to the Mouse Nest, a home for orphan mice. Grandfather Mouse and Fitch squeaked back and forth, and from time to time, the reeks of Ancient Mouse could be heard. This fascinated Homer, as he loved languages and had never known anyone who could speak Ancient Mouse.

At last they seemed ready to leave. So after several false starts—Uni forgot the booking calendar and La Biche forgot her straw hat—they were finally on their way!

By the time they arrived at the Three Corners fairgrounds, they had just enough time to drop off Homer's produce before they had to get in line at the baseball field for the parade. Homer and Fitch had never seen a parade. The floats were lining up, with the mayor and the Three Corners Cheese queen in the first car. The mayor, a rotund cheerful mouse who looked as if he never said no to a snack, was buttoning his vest and slicking back his whiskers as he positioned himself in the front seat of the red convertible. The cheese queen, a tall slender girl mouse with braces on her teeth and a puffy pink dress, was surrounded by several other teenage girl mice and several mouse mothers. They were helping her get seated on the top of the convertible's rear seat, fluffing her dress out around her and peppering her with instructions.

"Don't forget to smile, dear," said one of the mothers.

"Be sure to wave to both sides," said one of her friends.

"If they plan to stop, they'll tell you, so you can hold on," said her mother.

"Your hair is fine; you don't need to keep pulling on it," said another of her friends.

The cheese queen's mother arranged the bouquet of daisies in

73

her daughter's arms: first on the left side, then changing them to the right side—she was having a hard time making up her mind.

Fitch noticed an older male mouse in a colorful sport shirt and sandals, and he correctly assumed the mouse was the cheese queen's father. He kept trying to snap some pictures, but every time he got ready to click, someone else got in front of his daughter. "She looks good, Doris," he said to his wife. "Let me get a few photos." Then the mayor offered to take pictures of the queen and her parents together, and the arranging began again.

Fitch and Homer stood on the back of the rickshaw watching everything. They saw all the wonderful floats! Several looked like huge, orange chunks of cheese; another one had some cut-out trees and cardboard cows on it; and one, near the back, had a little merry-go-round on it, with several young mice from the local Junior Mouse Rangers troop demonstrating cat safety.

The fire whistle blew at 11:00 A.M. The marching band started to play, and the parade was off toward Main Street. La Biche opened the box of cellophane-wrapped peppermint twisters she had brought for everyone in the rickshaw to throw to the children. The crowd clapped as the rickshaw went past, and when the candy was tossed, they cheered even louder. All the children in the crowd rushed behind the rickshaw to pick up the candy treats.

Then Fitch saw them! He nearly fell out of the rickshaw. "Mom, Dad, Teddy, Sally, Freddy," he shouted, waving wildly while jumping up and down. Just at that moment, the parade stopped. A baton twirler in front of the band had lost her baton on a wild toss into the crowd. The unicorn signaled to Fitch's family to get into the rickshaw, which they were delighted to do! Fitch introduced Homer, La Biche and Uni to his family. After they had all hugged (and Grandfather Mouse had wiped his eyes and glasses again), the parade resumed. Everyone tossed out lots of sweets, and Fitch's mother squeezed his paw and gave him kisses on his head.

The last participants in the parade were the young ones on their bicycles: two-wheelers ridden by the teenagers, three-wheelers ridden by the grade-schoolers and bright plastic wagons filled with laughing, waving toddlers being pulled by their parents. The bicycles' wheels were all woven with crepe paper of every color; white, silver and blue streamers fluttered at the ends of the handle grips; and shiny whirligigs fastened to the backs of the seats spun and sparkled in the breeze.

The parade ended at Riverview Park. The crowd followed behind the bicycle brigade to the picnic area. Pennants and streamers gave the park a feeling of excitement. Grills had been set up and the smell of roasting sweet corn filled the air. The lemonade stand had a long line already, and La Biche took out her special sweet pink lemonade from the cooler in the rickshaw. It was still wonderfully cold, and the ice cubes were only slightly melted. Fitch rubbed his forehead with one cube and then moistened Homer's shell.

"Ahh, thanks a lot, Fitch," said Homer. "I really am hot! Do you think you could put me in a cool place for a while?"

"I'm taking my grandchildren over for a swim. Would you like to come too, Homer?" asked Grandfather Mouse.

"Do you think I could?" asked Homer, looking up at Uni for approval.

"Of course! Have a good swim, all of you. Fitch's parents, La Biche and I will prepare the picnic lunch. Come back in half an hour," said the unicorn, motioning them toward the swinging bridge and the swimming area.

No sooner was the picnic lunch prepared than it was eaten by the hungry swimmers. The afternoon had grown quite hot, so many of the adults retreated to the shade of the bingo tent. Others went to watch the judging of the produce contest, and the rest decided to catch a quick peaceful nap in a nearby grove of large trees.

At three o'clock, the three-legged cheese stool race began. Mice in teams of three went to the starting line. Each team had a three-legged cheese stool. The whistle blew, and one member of each team sat on the stool while the other two members picked up the stool and carried him as fast as they could. When the whistle sounded again, the teams set the stool down, the seated mouse stood up and moved to the left carry position, the left-side mouse moved to the right side, and the previous right-side mouse took a seat on the stool. As soon as this exchange had taken place, they were off toward the finish line, running as fast as they could. Soon the whistle blew again, and the exchange process repeated. The roots of this game went way back to ancient times, when Mouse Land was ruled by kings who were carried on thrones. Most of the stories about those ancient times were made up around the campfires now, because the truth was lost long ago. But the race was a lot of fun, and many of the mice had competed for years. Traditionally, the groups were formed of brothers, but sometimes it was just three mice who worked together or were good friends.

Uni and the rickshaw passengers stopped their activity to watch the race. Fitch's father and his two brothers had competed for many years. They had high hopes for this race, but unfortunately, the team in front of them stumbled at the second passenger exchange. The two teams fell in a heap together. The crowd gave out a group moan, but as no one was hurt, their attention quickly went back to the race. Fitch's dad and his brothers went back to their blanket in the shade to watch the rest of the race with their other family members, who gave them a round of applause for trying so hard. The mayor was soon announcing the winners, and the silver Three-Legged Cheese Stool Award was presented to this year's winners by the mayor and the cheese queen.

"Fitch, my son," Father Mouse said, "your uncles and I hope that honor will someday come to our family, but it may not happen until you, Freddy and Teddy are able to win it for us." He had one arm around Fitch's shoulders and the other around Teddy's. The boys hugged their father, laughing.

Uni finished giving all of her rickshaw rides at five o'clock. Just as she returned to their picnic spot, La Biche and Fitch's mother came back too. Homer was riding on La Biche's back, and tied to his shell was the largest first-place blue ribbon anyone had ever seen.

"He got first place for his novelty carrots," exclaimed La Biche. Homer ducked into his shell with embarrassment, but he soon came out again and everyone gave him three cheers. La Biche assisted the unicorn in unhooking the rickshaw, and then they tied the blue ribbon to the canopy so everyone could see it.

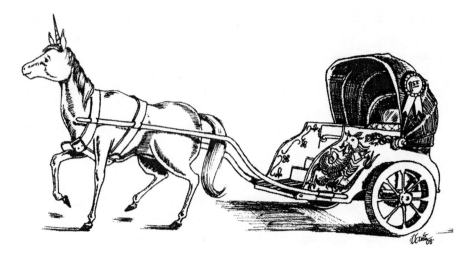

The big grills were in action again, and those who hadn't eaten too much cotton candy or too many cheese curds had some supper.

La Biche and Uni took a long walk after supper. Fitch noticed that they seemed to have something important to discuss, and he hoped it wasn't anything serious. When they came back, Uni was very quiet. Just as Fitch was going to ask if there was anything wrong, the first display of fireworks shot up into the sky. Everyone cheered and went down to the edge of the river so they could see the display reflected in the water. And what a display it was!

Fountains of white and blue filled the evening sky; whirligigs in red and green sparkled in groups and clusters. Several loud kabooms were heard, then the soft popping sounds of the fireworks that looked like dandelions and at last the hiss of the rocket finale.

Everyone cheered and clapped as the yellow cheese wedge shapes filled the sky one last time and then fell slowly toward the river.

The older children lit up their sparklers, and younger ones squeezed their toy spinners, which made sparks and funny whistling sounds.

The local families began saying good night to their friends as they gathered up their children, who were now chasing fireflies, and started to head for home. But many of the groups had come from far away to be part of the Cheese Festival, which had been a tradition for many years. These families were now putting up tents and rolling out sleeping bags, as they had done as children. They were preparing to camp out on the riverbank. A few campfires had been lit, and soon marshmallows were being passed around.

Fitch was thrilled that his group had decided to join all the families who were staying overnight to participate in the next day's festivities and that the adults had brought provisions for their camp out. Grandfather Mouse prepared their campfire, and it was now crackling and blazing brightly.

Fitch's mother kept busy wiping sticky marshmallow off of

everybody. "Do be careful," she admonished everyone, "or you'll all need baths before we can go to bed!"

La Biche had brought a special screened enclosure that she sometimes used to house her butterflies. She and Uni set it up for the whole mouse family, who unrolled their sleeping bags inside. Sally, Fitch's little sister, wanted to fill it with fireflies so she could have enough light to play with her dolls. Fitch just smiled at Uni and shook his head. She nodded and winked back.

Soon the campfires died down, and most of the happy company curled up in their tents or sleeping bags. Some of the older mice were still sitting up, telling stories about the Cheese Festivals of long ago. They surely would have started to make up very scary cat stories to frighten the little ones if the mouse mothers hadn't hurried the youngsters off to bed.

Uni and La Biche made themselves comfortable on the grass next to the screened tent. They stared up into the night sky and pointed out their favorite constellations: Cassiopeia, the Big Dipper, the North Star, and Orion.

Eventually, conversations faded and all that remained of the campfires was glowing red embers. Even La Biche had fallen asleep.

"Such a peaceful end to such an exciting day," Uni whispered to herself. Only one firefly was still awake with her, and it blinked its little yellow light on and off twice in agreement. Then it, too, went to sleep.

Chapter 8
The Secret

The sky was filled with purple and pink streaks, and the first stars could be seen as tiny specks. The sunset had been beautiful, and Fitch, Uni, Homer and La Biche were on their way back home after another long afternoon of rickshaw ride appointments. The afternoon had been hot, and the evening breeze felt very good as it rustled Fitch's fur. He leaned back on the cool leather seat, checking on the sleeping Homer beside him. He thought about the Cheese Festival and all the wonderful things he had experienced this weekend. The Sunday-morning pancake breakfast had been very special because three generations of his family had helped make the pancakes. The Cheese Festival Pancake Breakfast was a tradition. All the fathers and sons took over the grills, and it was a big fund-raiser for the Fire Department. Grandfather Mouse, Fitch's father and his older brother Teddy had won accolades for their teamwork. The pancakes had been delicious, with lots of butter and syrup.

Saying good-bye at the end of the day had been a bit sad for his mother and his little sister, but everyone agreed to write and get together for Thanksgiving. Grandfather Mouse had promised that Grandmother Mouse would be able to join them then, which made Fitch very happy, for he had missed her at this family reunion. His grandfather had explained that she had had to stay at their farm and tend to all the chores, but Fitch had sent his love to her through his grandfather, and he felt comforted knowing that his wishes would reach her and warm her heart.

Fitch closed his eyes so he could think more clearly, and he felt the rickshaw suddenly stop. Had they finally reached La Biche's cottage? He wanted to open his eyes to see what was happening, but his eyelids were very, very heavy. He could hear Uni and La Biche speaking in what sounded like an excited tone. His whiskers twitched. The wind had changed direction and it was much cooler now. He thought he heard thunder in the distance. His whiskers twitched again; he could smell the coming rain on the wind. He wanted to warn Uni and La Biche, but he was just too tired.

The next thing Fitch knew, they were on the brick path toward Temenos Inn. He could feel the bump, bump, bump of the bricks under the wheels of the rickshaw. He sat up just as large raindrops started to splatter down on the seat next to him. The toolshed door was open, and the unicorn got the rickshaw inside just in time. Moments later the clouds opened up and torrents of rain poured down on the roof and path.

"We'll just wait a few minutes. I'm sure this will let up," said Uni as she hung up the harness and began to wipe the rickshaw down with a clean rag. The rain pelted hard against the toolshed window.

"Summer storms are like this, but I'm sure Homer will be happy to have the moisture for the garden after such a hot spell," Uni continued while she and Fitch watched the rain cascade over the inn's eaves troughs and flood the path toward the garden. In a few minutes and after several more rumbles of thunder, the rain stopped as quickly as it had started.

"When I was little," Fitch said as they walked to the house in the last of the raindrops, "we ran out in the rain in our swimming suits and slid on the grass." The unicorn laughed quietly, and Fitch went on: "Of course, when our mother came home from choir practice, she was very upset with us. She was afraid we could have been hit by lightning. We hadn't thought of that, and we never thought to wake up our dad, who was asleep on the couch in the house. Oh, well, I guess it turned out all right." Fitch sighed with a smile, remembering how much fun he had had.

By the time the storm was over, it was dark outside. They carried Homer to his flowerpot bed, and then Uni put Fitch on her back and they went together down the front path to hang up the dragon lantern in the trellis. After that, they set about preparing a little snack before bed. They were very, very quiet so as not to wake Homer. They had decided to take their snack out on the porch.

"I have something very special to tell you and Homer," the unicorn whispered, "but it will have to wait until tomorrow since Homer is already asleep."

She clicked off the light in the kitchen, and they started to tiptoe away when a little voice said, "I'm awake. Please tell us the surprise, Uni."

Both Fitch and Uni stopped in their tracks. "I'm sorry we woke you, Homer. We were trying to be so quiet," said Fitch.

"Sorry, Homer," Uni added. "Would you like a little late-night snack?"

"Perhaps just a cool drink. But I'd love to know the secret!"

"Very well, I'll tell you both," said the unicorn as she took a homemade ice pop out of the freezer for Homer.

After they all got settled on the porch, Uni began. "As you may know, La Biche's family is from France. You may have noticed us talking quietly together over the past weeks. La Biche's French relatives wrote to her about a huge surprise birthday party that is being planned for her grandmother early next month. They are trying to get as many relatives to come as they can. Most of her family is local—La Biche is the only relative living out of the country. But she's definitely decided to attend, and we've been making special plans so we can all go with her."

Homer and Fitch were totally silent. "But how can we get there?" Fitch finally asked the same question that Homer had been thinking.

"Well, in my airplane," Uni replied, finishing her dish of strawberry ice cream.

"Your airplane!" they both said at once.

"I never noticed one around here," Fitch said, looking at Homer, who agreed with a little shrug.

"Oh," the unicorn said, laughing, "I don't keep it here! I keep it at the airport. I've been so busy since you boys came, I haven't had any time to go out flying."

The whole picture was finally beginning to form in Fitch's mind. "You mean we are going to have a trip? An airplane trip?" he squeaked with both hands on his cheeks. "To France? Oh, my goodness!" And he sat down very quickly on the porch step. Homer was too surprised to even curl up into his shell.

The unicorn scraped the very last of her ice cream out of her dish and chuckled. "I never thought it would be such a surprise for you. Shall we go take a look at the airplane tomorrow? I could take you up for a little ride if you like."

Fitch was ecstatic. He suggested that they all go to bed right away so they could get an early start tomorrow. Homer was very quiet and said something about needing to mist the ferns. But Fitch was excited enough for both of them. He asked Uni question after question while they prepared for bed. Uni got Homer all snuggled up back in his terra-cotta flowerpot. She had gathered a few fresh rose petals while they were on the porch, and Homer now settled down among them.

"Don't worry, Homer," said the unicorn, "it will be all right." Then she touched Homer's shell lightly with her horn. "Just have a good sleep now. We'll talk about things in the morning when you will feel a little more rested." Homer's eyes were heavy, and the unicorn watched him for a minute or two until he fell asleep.

Fitch was still asking Uni questions as he brushed his teeth upstairs. The news had invigorated him, and he was no longer sleepy. He had found his compass and was eager to show the unicorn how well he could use it. It was a wonderful handheld brass compass with a closeable case. Fitch's grandfather had given it to him with good instructions for its use.

They went into Uni's bedroom, where she took a large black leather case out of her closet. In the case were maps and manuals, two large green headsets, several notebooks and a foldable ruler. She spread all the contents out on her desk and looked carefully through the maps.

"Here's one we'll need for tomorrow," she said, pulling out a rather worn-looking map. They spread it out on the floor, and Fitch noticed that all sorts of blue lines had been drawn on it.

"That's what the ruler is for," explained the unicorn, unfolding it and placing it on the map. "There are lots of rules about airspace and flight patterns, but usually, we try to go in a straight line. We can use your compass to decide in which direction we should go for our trip tomorrow." Fitch and Uni worked over the maps for some time to get ready for their little trip. Every time she thought she had answered all his questions about flying, he would think of two or three more. "I think you will be a natural," she said as she tucked him into bed at last.

The first rays of the sunrise found the unicorn already in the garden. She had put the Chinese lantern back in the house, swept the path and porch and misted the ferns. By the time she returned inside, Homer was getting up.

"I picked the last blueberries," she said to Homer as she rinsed them under a stream of cold water. "Would you like some on your granola? Fitch was up very late last night, so I think we should eat our breakfast without him."

Homer agreed, and soon they were both crunching away. "You still seem a little anxious about our trip," the unicorn said in a soft voice.

Homer looked down at his bowl. Tears began to fill his eyes. The lump in his throat hurt, and he couldn't answer the unicorn.

"Let's go sit in the rocking chair," suggested Uni as she picked up Homer and gently carried him to the living room. She set him on the armrest that Fitch liked to sleep on, sat down herself and began to slowly rock. Homer's little antennae were drooping, and she could hear him sniff a little.

"Are you still remembering the bad day with the crows?" Homer nodded his agreement. "I'm sure that was a very scary experience, and we all know how brave you were to save your little brother. But we grow stronger with our ability to do things that are a little frightening to us. We really want you to come on our trip to France. I know you will enjoy it a lot. I have written to your parents to tell them about our plans. Why don't we just try to do this a little at a time? Just come along today and watch. Later in the week we can go to the airport again, as I have to begin to get the airplane ready for our long trip. Just see how you feel after today. Usually, when we understand our fears, they go away." They rocked a little longer.

"I'll give it a try," said Homer in a clear, strong voice. "I think I can do it."

"That's great," said the unicorn, touching him gently on his shell with her horn. "Shall we go finish our breakfast? Then we'll get Fitch up."

The weeks passed quickly as preparations for the trip were made. Homer started giving French lessons to Fitch and Uni every morning right after breakfast. The rickshaw ride schedule was cut back to afternoon and sunset rides only. Fitch did lots of map-plotting practice and started reading adventure books about flying in his spare time. La Biche and Homer made origami envelopes and readied many butterflies for the trip as a special surprise for La Biche's grandmother. Clothes were packed. Best of all, Homer started to enjoy riding in the airplane. He still closed his eyes during the landings, but Fitch was sure he had seen him start to open one eye a little bit. Letters went back and forth to Fitch's and Homer's families. Everyone was really excited about the upcoming adventure.

The last night at Temenos Inn was hectic. The rickshaw was packed with all the gifts and suitcases. The food coolers would be loaded on in the morning. Finally, everyone sat on the porch swing enjoying their last evening before the trip, trying to think of any last-minute items that might have been forgotten. Everyone was quite exhausted by all of the activities over the last few weeks.

"Well, I can't think of another thing," La Biche said after a while. "I think I'll go home now." She stood up to leave.

"I can't either," said the unicorn. "Shall we see you early?"

"I'll be here at sunrise to start out on our best adventure ever!" she said with a grin as she went down the path to the toolshed toward her shortcut home.

Teeth were brushed, faces washed and lights were out very quickly at Temenos Inn that night. "La Biche is right," thought Fitch. "Tomorrow will be the beginning of a really great adventure." He was still grinning when he fell asleep.

Chapter 9
Bon Voyage

"November 8336 Mike cleared for takeoff," said a deep, clear voice. Fitch's eyes popped open to see the unicorn standing next to his bed with a big smile on her face. It was still dark in Fitch's bedroom, but he could smell toast and he was sure there were cups of hot chocolate to go with it downstairs in the kitchen.

"Have I overslept?" he asked as he slipped out of his blanket and scurried around looking for his bathrobe.

"Not at all! It is still early. I just wanted us to all have a good breakfast together," said Uni, helping Fitch quickly make his bed. Then the two joined their friend downstairs.

"Good morning," said Homer, smiling and looking up from his apple slices sprinkled with cinnamon.

Fitch and Homer were clearing away the last of the dishes and Uni was on the telephone getting the weather report and checking the winds aloft when La Biche arrived at the kitchen door. The excitement was rising a little every minute as the food coolers were packed and loaded onto the rickshaw. Fitch was so excited as he scurried up and down to his bedroom, he kept forgetting what he had gone up to look for.

At last everything seemed in place on the rickshaw. Down the brick path and out the gate they all went. On the other side of the gate the unicorn stopped, unhooked her harness and went back toward Temenos Inn. Fitch watched and wondered what might have been forgotten. He saw the unicorn stop halfway down the path. She seemed to be pointing her horn at the toolshed, then at the house and then the garden. She nodded her head a little and tapped the ground with one of her golden hooves. The air became very still. It was just beginning to grow light, and the sky was pale blue with a dark orange glow just on the horizon. The sun would break up over the edge in a moment or two. The unicorn quickly returned to her position and rearranged the harness. In a moment, the whole company was turning right onto the road toward the airport.

Fitch gave Homer a little squeeze in his pocket. His own heart was beating very quickly with excitement. Fitch leaned over the armrest to look back at the sunrise, and he gasped with surprise! Temenos Inn seemed all fuzzy and misty. Fitch blinked and looked again. Now the toolshed, the garden, the trellis and finally the brick path began to disappear. Everything seemed to just fade out of sight. Through the mist, he could just make out a little sparkle of light, and then everything disappeared completely. Where a minute ago there had been buildings, now there was only a field of tall grass and a few trees. He rubbed his eyes and looked again. Temenos Inn was gone!

The sun had come up as a golden sliver of light behind the forest, which was now silhouetted in black in front of it. The sky was growing pink. Fitch turned to tell Uni and La Biche what he had seen. But just at that moment, the unicorn turned her head around, looked right at Fitch, and before he could speak, she winked. Fitch closed his mouth and didn't say a word. He felt all warm inside as he nestled into the leather seat. The unicorn looked back at him again for just a moment, and they exchanged quiet smiles.

The weeks before the trip had seemed to Fitch to pass very slowly, but the morning of their departure was passing very quickly. Soon they were at the airport. The large hangar doors were rolled open, and Uni and La Biche carefully pushed the airplane out on the tarmac. La Biche took over the inspection. She carefully inspected every detail, calling them out to Fitch, who checked the items off on his clipboard. Oil and gasoline, wing surfaces, rudder and tires were all carefully inspected. The unicorn had gone into the airport office to file their flight plan. Everyone was soon aboard, with seat belts fastened.

The unicorn opened her window. "Clear," she shouted, and then Fitch's heart jumped into his throat as the engine came to life and the propeller started to turn. Homer, who had been on Fitch's shoulder during all the preparations, rolled himself into his shell and dropped into the pocket of Fitch's shirt. Fitch lightly patted the pocket.

"November 8336 Mike, you are cleared for takeoff on runway zero nine zero. Have a good trip," crackled through the radio.

"Roger, tower," said the unicorn as she finished her run-up at the end of the taxiway and started rolling to the end of the runway. Checking the weather sock to be sure they would be flying into the wind, she guided the airplane to the centerline of the runway. She turned to look at Fitch, who gave her a thumbs-up. The unicorn advanced the throttle to full. The airplane quickly gained speed as it rolled down the runway toward the rising sun. With no effort at all, the wheels left the ground. Fitch heard the thump of the wheels as they were folded up into their storage place and then the thud of the storage doors closing. The airport was behind them now, becoming a smaller and smaller spot on the ground. They were quite high and still climbing. Uni and La Biche exchanged a few words from time to time as Uni adjusted the trim with the little wheel by the side of her seat. They really were on their way to France at last!

The weather was perfect for flying. Fitch was in charge of doling out food and drinks from the coolers. They sang songs, played word games, and Fitch and Homer took naps and practiced their string games. Fitch said the time passed in anticipation, like waiting for your birthday, and everyone agreed. Fitch had dozed off again when Homer, looking out of the window from his place on Fitch's shoulder, started to speak in an excited voice.

"*Nous sommes arrivés,*" he said in French. "I mean, we are over France!" he translated.

Fitch roused himself and pushed his face against the window. Uni tipped the wing a little so he could see out better. Below, a few little fluffy clouds scuttled away to reveal tiny farms on green and brown squares of land. Thin roads wound around the patches of green. Fitch noticed several craggy mountains sticking up to the far right just as La Biche asked, "Do you see the mountains over there? That is the Pic St. Loup. My grandmother lives just below it."

Fitch could tell how excited La Biche was by the tone of her voice. She had explained one evening, while they all sat on the porch, that she hadn't seen her grandmother for many years. She and her brother, Jean-Claude, had been raised by their grandmother in her little country home in southern France.

Fitch could see the Pic St. Loup getting closer and closer. Suddenly, he saw a pair of very slim planes circling high above the mountains. The unicorn was busy on the radio as she and La Biche began running through their landing checklist. Fitch stared at the two planes, which soared on the winds above the Pic St. Loup. Homer had noticed them too. Almost as if he had read Fitch's mind, Homer said, "They are gliders."

"Oh, of course!" said Fitch with a gasp of understanding. "I read about them. They don't have motors and are towed up in the air by regular airplanes, then they're cut loose to ride the silent air currents." They watched as the gliders swooped down and then, catching a warm airstream, were carried off into the distance again.

"Wow," they said together as they both turned and laughed.

"I think we should get Uni to arrange a ride for us," said Homer.

"That's just what I was thinking," said Fitch, but he was surprised at Homer's desire to do something so challenging.

"I have always wondered what a hot-air balloon ride would be like," said Homer in a sort of musing tone. Fitch noticed Uni and La Biche turn and look at each other at Homer's comment. They were probably as surprised as he was at this change in Homer.

The unicorn was on the final leg of the landing, and the plane touched down smoothly. Before long, the supplies were unpacked, the airplane tied down and the rickshaw reassembled. The unicorn harnessed herself up, and, with maps checked, the company started off toward Grandma Biche's house.

Homer had read several guidebooks on the region. As they traveled, he began to explain that this area of France had been under an ancient sea and that was why there were so many limestone mountains and hills. "I hope we have time to collect some specimens and look for fossils," said Fitch. The short bushes and small oak trees gave way to little grassy fields mixed with neat rows and rows of grapevines.

Suddenly, La Biche shouted, "Stop! There's her mailbox!"

Indeed, hidden between two fields of grapevines was a worn gravel path. The unicorn made a quick left turn down the path and stopped. A dog barked in the distance. La Biche hopped out of the rickshaw and hurried on ahead of the company. Fitch looked and looked, but all he could see were rows of deep green vines heavy with green or purple grapes. All at once the red tiles of a roof could be seen above the vines, then a limestone house with yellow shutters appeared. It was just as La Biche had described it: several large windows to let in the light, a fig tree by the door and two huge plane trees to shade the house in the summer. Fitch's sharp eyes noticed three bee boxes under the oak trees in the garden area. Just like in La Biche's garden!

The dog, which Fitch had heard barking, was at the gate, and La Biche was reaching between the wrought-iron bars of the gate to pet him. His tail wagged in greeting as the rickshaw stopped.

"Grandmère, Grandmère," called La Biche. *"C'est moi, ta biche."*

Down the path from the house came a tall, pale brown deer. Her coat had many white hairs, especially around her face, and she was wearing gold-rimmed glasses. She seemed a little hesitant at first, and then Fitch remembered this was a surprise visit. La Biche reached inside the gate and unhooked the latch, and soon she and her grandmother were running toward each other. The dog took advantage of the open gate to come out and investigate the unicorn, the rickshaw and its contents. He seemed like a kind dog, and it only took a moment for the unicorn to confirm that for Homer and Fitch. Grandma Biche happily nuzzled La Biche on her nose and neck for a long time.

Introductions were quickly made. Fitch was grateful that

Grandma Biche spoke English as well as French. She had a kind face

and a warm, comforting voice. Like his own grandfather, she had to wipe her eyes and clean her glasses several times on her apron at such a happy and exciting reunion. Soon everything was unpacked, and the rickshaw was stored in the garage next to the house. La Biche and Uni carried their two small friends into the orchard, where Grandma Biche had been gathering apples in a large basket before their arrival. The trees were full, and the branches were hanging very low to the ground. The warm smells of late summer filled the air, and a few busy bees droned past on their way to their hives.

"After our lunch, we will finish gathering the Reinette apples. I will store them for several months until they mature. They are very delicious in the winter," said Grandma Biche.

"We could go finish that task," volunteered La Biche. "A good stretch would feel great after such a long trip." So out they went with several baskets.

Grandma Biche was very busy in the kitchen while the apples were being gathered. By the time the apples were collected, she had laid a wonderful table of treats: fresh, warm applesauce with cinnamon; crusty French bread; *pain au chocolate* (chocolate bread); four or five selections of cheese; tarts with nut fillings; and a large pitcher of dark, rich hot chocolate. Fitch couldn't get over all the wonderful cheeses, and the crusty bread was unlike anything he had ever tasted.

The kind dog placed himself in the doorway with his head on his outstretched paws. Fitch thought that he took his job as a guard dog very seriously. From time to time, he would lift up his head or point his ears to check if anything was going on that needed his attention. His long, shiny black coat gave him an air of authority and strength, but Fitch noticed that his eyes were gentle and that the patch of white fur under his chin gave away his softer side.

The mazet, which Grandma Biche explained was what her type of house was called, had been built many years ago in the vineyard to store the vine grower's sprayer and tractor. When she bought it those many years ago, it had been in ruins and covered with brambles.

La Biche said she remembered her mother telling stories about rebuilding the thick limestone walls.

"We will make a fire in the fireplace if it gets cool this evening," said Grandma Biche.

"Do you remember the stories you told Jean-Claude and me when we very young?" asked La Biche.

Grandma Biche smiled and nuzzled La Biche's neck. "Of course I do," she said gently.

Just then the kind dog jumped to his feet, barked and started off at a run for the gate. "What's the matter, Nico?" asked La Biche as everyone left the table and followed him down the path. Fitch snatched up Homer, who had quickly retreated into his shell. Fitch knew Homer would be curious once he stopped being alarmed.

By the time they reached the gate, loads of La Biche's relatives were piling out of their cars and running toward them. Cousins, uncles and aunts, nephews and nieces—all excitedly speaking in French—hugged and kissed La Biche and Grandma Biche. Nico circled the large group, wagging his tail in excited expectation that perhaps someone might have brought a doggie treat. Fitch, Homer and Uni were introduced to all the family members, and then a happy round of hugs and kisses started all over again. La Biche explained that in some parts of France, it is customary to give two small kisses, one on each cheek; but in southern France, where they were, everyone gives three. Fitch thought this was a great idea. Homer, who was really too tiny to receive kisses from all the relatives, smiled and bowed his antennae while he got little pats on his shell. This seemed to make everyone feel included and happy.

It wasn't long before everybody helped to put up tables under the pergola, which were then spread with yellow tablecloths and mountains of food. The family's car trunks had been filled with baskets and baskets of goodies to eat. Grandma Biche went inside to start a fire in the fireplace for later, and just as the embers began to glow in the outdoor grills set up for roasting vegetables, a bicyclist came up the path. His sleek, colorful outfit, helmet and sunglasses prevented La Biche from recognizing him at first, but after he handed her several long, thin, crisp loaves of bread he had been carrying, he removed his sunglasses.

"Jean-Claude!" shouted La Biche, and she threw herself around her brother. He laughed and hugged her so hard, he lifted her off the ground.

Fitch could see tears welling up in Homer's eyes just before he retreated into his shell. La Biche had spoken about her brother many times in the evenings as they sat on the porch at Temenos Inn. He was in business and traveled a lot, but they hadn't seen each other for a long time. La Biche had given Fitch and Homer the stamps from his letters, which were often from places they had to look for on the unicorn's globe.

Now the reunion was complete. The conversations and stories went on long into the evening. Plans were laid for trips, and secret whispering went on whenever Grandma Biche went into the mazet to fix more food or restock the fireplace for the youngsters. The unicorn brought out a bag of marshmallows from the cooler. Fitch showed the cousins, nieces and nephews how to toast them on sticks. At first they just watched, as they had never seen this before, but soon everyone was trying their hand at it. Several marshmallows caught on fire and one or two fell into the flames, but Homer and Fitch explained that it was just part of the fun.

Sticky, full, laughing but tired, the younger relatives started to rub their eyes and yawn. Soon they were standing quietly next to their parents. It was time for everyone to go home. Jean-Claude hugged La Biche and Grandma Biche as he said good night. He was the last to leave, but he promised to be back in the morning.

"On ne sait pas ce que demain nous reserve," said Grandma
Biche as she stood in the doorway with Nico beside her, waving
good-bye to Jean-Claude.

"What did she say?" whispered Fitch, wishing he had studied a little harder.

"You never know what tomorrow will bring," translated Homer with a smile.

Lovely beds were prepared for Fitch and Homer on the thick stone windowsill in the kitchen: a small flowerpot for Homer lined with wild thyme and an empty wooden Camembert cheese box for Fitch. Fitch loved the smell. La Biche was out closing all the shutters, which Grandma Biche explained was the custom in France. When La Biche got to the kitchen shutters, she left one open partway so Homer and Fitch would see the Pic St. Loup as soon as the sun came up. Grandma Biche slept near the fireplace now, since, she explained to Uni, it was too difficult to climb the stairs to the loft on a regular basis. The twin beds up there were always ready, as she never knew when she would have visitors. Everyone laughed as she hugged and kissed them all good night. Even Nico was exhausted after so much excitement. He soon had his head on his paws as he stretched out on his rug in front of the fireplace.

The mazet was very quiet with nearly everyone sound asleep. Fitch looked up at the Pic St. Loup, a soft dark form rising up to meet the moon. A bright star was shining just to the left of the mountain.

"That must be a planet. I'll have to ask Homer," he started to think,

and then he, too, joined the sleeping house.

Chapter 10
A Day of Surprises

"Fitch, Fitch, Fitch! Wake up!" Homer was shaking Fitch as hard as he could. "You'll never believe what's happening," he went on in the most excited voice he could manage. Fitch sat up and rubbed his eyes. Homer was sitting on the edge of his cheese box bed peering out of the window, his antennae waving wildly.

"What is it, Homer?" Fitch asked through a stretch and a yawn. He rubbed his eyes again and stood up in his bed. As he stretched his tail, he looked out the window and gasped. He saw the most incredible sight he had ever seen! All around Grandma Biche's mazet, down the lane and in the fields surrounding the house, were sheep, hundreds and hundreds of sheep—sheep of every size; big woolly rams with horns and mother ewes with baby lambs; white, black and brown sheep, sheep, sheep, sheep! Many of them had red wool pom-poms on their collars. Others had blue paint sprayed in a design on their backs. The air was full of their bleating as the mothers tried to keep track of their babies or find their friends in the huge group. The bells, which many of them had around their necks, clanked cheerfully as the flock moved past the window.

Fitch and Homer had their noses pressed against the glass. They were speechless at the sight. Fitch noticed one of the shepherds leaning on his staff and talking to La Biche and Jean-Claude at the gate.

Just then a large brown ewe caught Fitch's attention. She had stopped by the huge plane tree that was next to the kitchen window. Fitch started to tell Homer that he had never seen brown sheep, even in books, but he stopped speaking right in the middle of his sentence because now there were two sheep in front of his eyes, and then a moment later there were three. The mother ewe had just had twins!

The shepherd stopped talking to La Biche and Jean-Claude. He came over to the plane tree and was soon helping the twin lambs stand up on their new shaky legs. He noticed Homer and Fitch in the window and motioned for them to come outside. La Biche went into the house right then to be sure they were not missing this exciting morning. As Fitch pulled on his jeans and T-shirt, La Biche explained that the event they were witnessing was called "transhumance"—the time of year when shepherds gather their flocks together from the summer mountain pastures and return them to their winter homes at the local farms. She explained that three families were bringing their sheep home, that they had left the mountains several days ago and that there were about eight hundred sheep in this group. Some years, when the weather was bad, the sheep had to be brought down in trucks, but this year they were able to use the centuries-old tradition of herding them down the roads and through the villages. "But I think the walk is over for this mother and her babies," said La Biche.

And sure enough, as she spoke, a small green van pulled up to assist the new family. Both babies were having some milk from their mother. Fitch and Homer hopped on La Biche's back and outside they went. After greeting Jean-Claude and getting all the customary kisses, they were introduced to the shepherd, Monsieur Richard, and his son, Olivier, who was now getting the new family into the little van. Homer looked distressed that these animals were being separated from their flock. As for the two lamb twins themselves, they took turns bleating, and this seemed to stir up the six or seven other baby lambs in the van. Fitch couldn't believe the noise.

"The rest of the herd will find these sheep safe and sound when they get to the big barn tonight. Don't worry, they always get back together!" Monsieur Richard said with a chuckle. Homer smiled at that and seemed much happier.

"We'd better be going," said the shepherd in French.

Fitch was so happy he had understood him well enough to answer, *"Merci et au revoir,"* which was the best he could do. Homer congratulated him quietly on his effort.

Just as the herd was moving away, Grandma Biche's large blue car came down the lane. She and Uni had gone to the village for bread, vegetables and pastries for lunch. Monsieur Richard and the

other shepherds tipped their caps to Grandma Biche, and the flock of bleating sheep slowly started down the road toward Ste. Croix de Quintillargue, a nearby village. By the time the car was unpacked, the last of the sheep could barely be seen in the distance, but the tinkling of their bells was still audible for a long time.

When Fitch went back into the house, he was surprised to see a pile of wild mushrooms on the table. La Biche was busy cleaning and cutting them up. Fitch got up on the kitchen chair to watch but couldn't contain his concern. "My mother never let us eat wild mushrooms," he said rather abruptly. Surprised at the forwardness of his comment, he cleared his throat and added with a shy smile, "Do you think they are safe?"

La Biche took his comment very seriously, and Homer, too, lifted his head and waited for her answer. "We only collect mushrooms we recognize from places we know," she began, "and then we take them to the pharmacy. The pharmacist identifies and checks them for us."

"Really?" said Fitch, amazed.

"Yes. Everyone in France knows they can do that, and we are very careful to always check. These are called 'grisette' by the local people."

"That would be *Amanita vaginata* in Latin," said Homer, "but you could translate grisette as 'little grays.'"

"Wait until I translate it all into a wonderful cream sauce for our fresh pasta," said Grandma Biche with a twinkle in her eye. Everyone agreed that would be the best idea of all.

After the wonderful lunch Grandma Biche made with the wild grisette mushrooms and the great pastries they had brought from the village, everyone scattered to attend to various chores. Homer and Fitch retired to take a little nap. But Fitch had barely closed his eyes when an enormous noise filled the lane outside the house. He jumped to his feet and looked out of the window. A huge machine and several small tractors, each with high-sided wagons, pulled up and stopped. Several men got out of a small white van, and a lot of conversation followed. Hands were waved and several bunches of grapes were examined by someone Fitch thought must be the owner of the vineyard.

After a while, the large man in dark green overalls, who had been driving the strange machine climbed back in his rig and closed the cab door. From his position high up in the machine, he could see the whole field, and Fitch wondered what that strange noisy machine would do. The man in the cab positioned the machine at the end of a row of grapevines. Gears were changed, and after several false starts, the machine began to whir and a conveyor belt with many soft vinyl cups started to rotate. It was a grape-picking machine!

Down the row of vines went the huge machine. It gently shook the vines until the soft, ripe grapes dropped off the stems and fell into the plastic cups. These cups carried the grapes up to two bins on the top of the picker machine. The grapes were quickly dumped out of the cups, freeing the cups to return for more of the fruit. Down one row and back up the next row went the strange picker machine. When it

was back up by the lane, one of the smaller tractors brought its wagon

up, and the machine's storage bins raised to meet it, dumping the

grapes into the waiting wagon. With the storage bins now empty, the

grape-picking machine started down another row.

Fitch turned to wake up Homer, whom he thought was asleep

in his flowerpot bed, but Homer was awake, watching the process

with a fixed gaze. The two laughed and continued to watch for a long

time. They were fascinated by the quick progress the machine made.

Before long, the first wagon full of grapes was driven away down the

lane, then a second one pulled up. By the time it was full, the first one

was back again.

"Would like to see where the wagons are going?" asked Uni. Fitch jumped. He had been so engrossed in watching the grape harvest that he hadn't even noticed Uni entering the room. "Sorry, I didn't mean to startle you."

"Do you think we could follow them?" asked Homer.

"I was going to say we could hook up the rickshaw and follow them to the winery."

The unicorn put her head down close to Homer and Fitch and whispered, "Jean-Claude, La Biche and I want to go get Grandma Biche's birthday gift, so this might give us an opportunity to slip away to do that," and she winked at them both.

Fitch could see Grandma Biche sweeping the ashes out of the fireplace with Jean-Claude's help. Fitch cleared his throat rather loudly and said, "I think we should all go to visit the winery, Uni, and see where those grapes are going."

La Biche, who had been peeling apples for a tart, looked up. "I haven't been to the winery for many years. I would love to go along and say hello to our neighbors there."

Jean-Claude was ready now to carry the basket of ashes out to

the garden. He turned and grinned mischievously at Fitch and Homer.
"I could drive you in Grandma's car if you like," he said. "Could we
take the car, Grandmère? Would you like to come along?"

Everyone held their breath in case Grandma Biche said yes.

"No, no. You go along to see to the grapes. I want to bake the
pies, and then I plan to relax in the garden with a cup of mint tea. This
has all been very exciting!" La Biche and Jean-Claude hugged
Grandma Biche in reply. Soon she was wiping her gold-rimmed
glasses on her apron again.

Fitch and Homer got ready quickly, and within minutes, they were going down the lane in Grandma Biche's big blue car. Nico's tail wagged as Grandma Biche closed the gate and waved them off.

At the winery, one of the wagons full of red grapes had just arrived and was waiting for its load to be dumped into the press. The air was heavy with the smell of fermenting grapes. Monsieur Thibault, Grandma Biche's neighbor who ran the winery, was delighted to see Jean-Claude and La Biche. After introductions were made to the rest of the party, Monsieur Thibault took them all into the large building behind the area where the grapes were being dumped. Huge brown oak vats, which almost reached the ceiling, were arranged along one wall, and several equally huge shiny stainless-steel vats stood along the opposite wall. Homer and Monsieur Thibault got on very well, and soon they were chattering on in French so quickly that Fitch couldn't follow the conversation at all.

La Biche suggested to Fitch that they go up to the house and say hello to Madame Thibault. So they slipped away and left Uni with Homer and Monsieur Thibault, who were deep in discussion on the advantages of oak barrels.

123

Like Monsieur Thibault, Madame Thibault was warm and friendly. A short, smiling woman in a yellow flowered dress and shawl, she welcomed La Biche and Fitch into her kitchen, where she was preparing large pots of wonderfully smelling leek-and-potato soup. La Biche presented her with a basket of quince fruit from Grandma Biche, and Madame Thibault refilled the basket with pomegranates as a birthday gift for Grandma Biche.

It seemed to Fitch that only moments had passed before they were all back in the big blue car, waving good-bye to the Thibaults. More wagonloads of grapes had arrived, and things had become very busy at the winery.

"Where are we going now?" asked Fitch.

"To watch Grandma Biche's birthday present being made," answered Jean-Claude as he pulled onto the main road.

"Does everyone know the secret except Homer and me?" said Fitch, pretending to pout.

"Yeah," said Homer, joining in the fun and making his antennae as defiant as he could.

"We are off to Claret," said Uni, laughing at Fitch, who now had his arms crossed as well as his lips puckered.

"Claret!" squeaked Fitch.

"The glassmaking center of this region," said Homer excitedly.

"Why, yes," said La Biche. "How did you know that?"

Both Homer and Fitch started to talk at once: "We read about it before we left home. We really wanted to go there. Do you think they will be making things today?"

"We have an appointment with a master craftsman," said Jean-Claude.

"He will be making a special gift for Grandma Biche. We have been writing to him for months, and he will make her gift today," finished La Biche.

The countryside was very beautiful, with many rows of grapevines heavy with grapes. Fitch noticed that many of the vineyards were still being harvested by crews of pickers rather than by the strange machines. Jean-Claude explained that years ago all the grapes were picked by hand, but now it was difficult to find people who would do such hard work, so the machines were getting more popular. Beautiful old buildings filled each of the little villages they passed through, and their window boxes overflowed with cascades of flowers.

Claret, an ancient center for glassmaking, was not very large. Jean-Claude parked the car on one of the narrow side streets. A small sign over what looked like an old garage showed a man blowing on a long tube with a ball of glass on the end. Under the picture it said: HENRI ST. BAUZILLE SUR RENDEZ-VOUS.

The unicorn rang the bell. A young man answered the door. Jean-Claude explained who they were, and the young man showed them into the workshop. It was a large room with a high ceiling. The walls were lined with shelves on one side, which held many beautiful glass pieces. Vases, bowls, stemmed glasses and elegant pitchers in bright sparkling colors made the wall glow with light. In the center of the room was a large red-hot furnace with a half-opened door. Fitch saw the heat waves coming out of the opening.

An elderly gentleman in a blue smock and a beret laid down a tool he had been cleaning, and with a large smile, he came over and hugged La Biche and Jean-Claude. His long white hair had been held back by his beret, but as he took it off to greet them, his tresses fell forward over his shoulders. His face was deeply wrinkled, and his hands looked large for his frame. The knuckles, too, were large, but when the man shook hands with Fitch, they felt soft and surprisingly gentle. He had a warm smile and a welcoming voice. After a little conversation, he showed them to an observation area, where they could safely and comfortably watch him work. Homer sat on Fitch's shoulder.

Monsieur St. Bauzille returned to his workbench and began. The long metal pipe with a huge ball of glass on the end was placed in the furnace. As it began to soften, it was rolled from side to side to keep it centered on the pipe. The young man was Monsieur St. Bauzille's assistant and, Homer figured, also an apprentice. He and the master glassmaker made a perfect team.

Soon the glass was ready to be blown and shaped. In and out of the furnace it went. Blowing and rolling the pipe on a special wooden edge, the glass ball soon started to take a shape. Colored patterns were worked into the sides, and little by little, a beautiful bowl was created right before their eyes. Wet newspapers were used to form and shape the creation, and then, with a *pop,* Monsieur St. Bauzille took the bowl off the pipe and set it on the table.

He continued to work the edges until everyone was able to see what the colored swirls were: They were butterflies—wonderful, colorful butterflies! Fitch and Homer marveled at the finished product. A large clear glass fruit bowl adorned with wonderful orange, red, white and yellow butterflies stood before them— absolutely the perfect gift for Grandma Biche.

Monsieur St. Bauzille came out of the work area, and everyone shook his hand and complimented him on the lovely bowl. Homer translated to Fitch that Monsieur St. Bauzille offered to bring the gift to the party himself, and everyone thought that was a good plan since, secretly, no one wanted to be responsible in case it broke in transit.

Just then the apprentice came over to the group; he had two small gifts for Fitch and Homer. He presented a lovely green glass snail to Homer and a tiny mouse to Fitch. Everyone thanked and praised the young man for his fine work. He blushed and excused himself. Monsieur St. Bauzille explained that he had instructed the young man to practice such tiny projects regularly and that he thought the apprentice showed a lot of promise.

The sun had already slipped behind the Pic St. Loup by the time the big blue car turned down the lane to the mazet. It was time to close the shutters and give Nico his supper.

Fall was in the air tonight, and Grandma Biche had built another wonderful fire in the stone fireplace. It sparked and crackled and gave a warm glow to the limestone walls of the house.

Dinner dishes were quickly done, and everyone said the apple tart dessert was the best they had ever eaten.

Jean-Claude and La Biche went up to the loft, but they quickly returned with three small cases. When opened, they were lined with dark blue velvet and each one held a silver flute. It took a little coaxing, but soon Grandma Biche and her grandchildren were sorting through a stack of sheet music trying to decide which pieces to play.

Uni explained to Homer and Fitch that Grandma Biche had been a concert flutist, and after she had retired, she gave lessons to most of the youngsters in the area and, of course, to her grandchildren.

Homer and Fitch got ready for bed, as they knew they would get sleepy once the three musicians began to play. Grandma Biche came over to the windowsill to make sure they were comfortable and to wish them good night. "You never know what tomorrow will bring," she said as she gave them both a kiss.

The wonderful clear notes of the three musicians' flutes soon filled the mazet. "This lullaby is a lovely end to a perfect day," thought Fitch. Uni rocked gently in Grandma Biche's rocking chair. Fitch looked at the moon over the Pic St. Loup. Homer was already asleep. Fitch snuggled under his quilt and let the music carry him to dreamland.

Chapter 11
Up, Up and Away

Grandma Biche was up very early the next morning. In fact, by the time Fitch woke up, three pans of brioche were sitting on the counter next to him. Each was covered with a damp, white tea towel. The contents of the pans were on their last rise before being baked. The smell of fresh rolls would soon fill the air, and Fitch stayed under his quilt a few more minutes imagining the butter melting on the warm, golden brown breakfast treats.

"Good morning, sleepyhead," said Homer, who had just appeared at the end of Fitch's bed.

"Good morning, Homer," said Fitch as he yawned and stretched his tail. "Where is everyone?" he asked with a shrug.

"La Biche and Uni left very early before anyone was up. I only heard the door close and then saw them through the window as they went out the gate. Grandma Biche is hanging up laundry, and I have been examining the rocks we collected." The windowsill was covered in rock samples, which Homer had gathered during their

131

visit. His magnifying glass was up on its little stand. A large, leather-bound text about rocks and minerals was open next to it.

"I've borrowed Grandma Biche's book," he said. "Did you know she used to do some speleology when she was younger?"

Fitch sat on the edge of his bed staring at his feet.

"She has a number of excellent samples that she's going to give me to take home," Homer went on, his voice getting more excited with every word. "She once—"

Fitch scratched his head and interrupted his friend's speech. "Wait a minute. What is spely who?"

"Speleology. You know, the study of caves. There are lots of caves around here, and Grandma Biche has been to most of them. That means she was a spelunker—that's what you call someone who explores caves. I would love to go into a cave," Homer said with a faraway sound in his voice. "Remember I said this region had been under an ancient ocean?"

Fitch was still sitting on the side of his bed and sort of looking for his tail warmer.

"I've found lots of fossil remains in these limestone samples. I've done several sketches, and I think I have identified most of them," Homer continued as he motioned Fitch to come over and look. But then Homer stopped talking for a moment and looked at Fitch. "Maybe you should have a little breakfast first."

Fitch slowly slid off the bed. He had spotted his T-shirt. The tail warmer was under it. Fitch smiled at Homer. "I would love to hear all about it, but you're right, a little bit of breakfast first."

Just then Grandma Biche came in with a dusty box and an empty laundry basket.

Fitch pulled the quilt up on his bed as Homer and Grandma Biche began chatting away in French. Soon Fitch had a large steaming bowl of hot chocolate in front of him and the pans of brioche were in the oven giving off a most heavenly smell. He decided not to have toast with fig jam or chestnut honey, both of which he now loved a lot, but to wait for the fresh brioche to be baked.

Nico, who had been lying in the doorway again, suddenly stood up and barked. He was quickly off down the path to the gate to welcome La Biche and Uni home. As they came in the mazet, Fitch noticed that La Biche seemed to be suppressing a smile and that their whispered conversation quickly turned to a louder discussion of car

133

engines and bicycles. In a quiet moment, Uni gave Fitch and Homer a quick wink and a nod to indicate that she would like to have a private word with them. La Biche asked Grandma Biche for her brioche recipe. Seemingly full of questions, she took up her place at the table with pen and paper; and Grandma Biche became so busy explaining all the recipe details, she never noticed when Fitch and Homer got on Uni's back and went outside.

Fitch giggled as Uni walked out into the orchard. "Tell us, tell us," they said together, bursting with excitement.

The unicorn stood under one of the low-slung pear trees. Fitch climbed off onto a branch. He set Homer on a twig beside him, and they both anxiously waited to hear what Uni wanted to tell them.

"We went off to the village for a big meeting this morning," she began. "The mayor and several council members from the area have organized a wonderful surprise for Grandma Biche. As you know, she was well known for her concert work, and then she earned a wonderful reputation for the flute lessons she gave for many years to the young folks in all the villages of this region. Some of those students have gone on to be famous and successful in the music world. As a tribute to her, each of the villages wants to have a celebration in its town square this afternoon. Our problem was how to get Grandma Biche from location to location quickly, and then Homer gave us an idea."

"I did?" said Homer with a quizzical look.

"Yes, but you probably didn't know you had at the time," said the unicorn. "Remember you mentioned wanting to take a hot-air balloon ride while we were landing here?"

"I remember that," said Fitch. "We were watching the gliders when you said it!"

Homer seemed to recall now, but he still looked puzzled.

Fitch slapped his forehead with his paw. "Of course," he burst out. "What a perfect idea!"

Homer began to smile as he looked up at the sky. "And you have the perfect day for it."

"Indeed so," said Uni. "We have made all the final arrangements. Now we just have to get Grandma Biche ready without ..."

"Letting the cat out of the sack," snickered Fitch, finishing the unicorn's statement.

All three of the conspirators giggled at Fitch's comment and at the prospect of getting something over on Grandma Biche. Then Uni continued confiding the plan: "La Biche is telling her right now that we have arranged for Monsieur Seuffert to come at two o'clock to take a family portrait. That way, she will get dressed in her best outfit for the photo. Many of the nephews and nieces and cousins are in fact coming around three o'clock to help with the balloon lines when it arrives. We will have to hold it down while she gets in. After she is up and away, we can set up the decorations here in the garden for the birthday party afterward."

Nico came bounding out into the orchard with La Biche, who called them to come in and eat fresh brioche. She exchanged a few quick words with the unicorn, who whispered to Fitch and Homer, "It is all arranged."

Just as the brioche cooled enough to eat, Nico jumped to his feet and ran with a quick bark to the gate. Jean-Claude had arrived.

More hot chocolate was made, oranges were squeezed, and in no time at all, everyone enjoyed the tantalizing meal.

While the table was being cleared, Homer had a moment to quietly remind La Biche to take the butterflies out of the cooler so

136

they could warm up and be ready to fly when the party started. In the excitement, La Biche had nearly forgotten, and she thanked Homer several times in a very quiet voice.

Homer then engaged Grandma Biche in the rock samples. She opened the dusty box that she had brought in from the shed. It was filled with pieces of stalactites and stalagmites and also an album of old photos. Fitch joined in the discussion, and it was easy for Uni, La Biche and Jean-Claude to slip outside and start the decorations. After a while, Fitch crept away from the conversation for a moment to peek outside and see how the decorations were going. He was surprised to see that the garden was nearly ready. Tiny lights were strung along the pergola. Several folding tables had been set up with folding chairs, all of which had been hidden behind Nico's doghouse. Flowers were placed in vases and set on the tables, which were covered with crisp white paper. He couldn't believe how the garden had been transformed. Jean-Claude was just finishing the test of the fairy lights in the trees. They were still flickering on and off. Fitch felt Nico getting restless behind him, so he quickly went back to the geology discussion, although he did manage to give Homer a secret thumbs-up sign.

Before long, La Biche reminded everyone that Monsieur Seuffert would be there soon. Coats were brushed and outfits changed for the pictures. Suddenly, Nico barked and raced to the gate again. Monsieur Seuffert had arrived. Fitch stopped dead in his tracks when he went out the door. The garden looked exactly as it always did. No lights, no tables, no flowers in vases.

"Does the view remind you of Temenos Inn?" said a soft voice behind him.

"Why, yes, it does," Fitch answered in a whisper as he accepted a ride on the unicorn's back.

Greetings and embraces were exchanged. In fact, two photographers had arrived. Monsieur Seuffert Jr., a serious young man, rather tall for his age and wearing glasses, was unloading equipment from their car. Monsieur Seuffert Sr., a distinguished gentleman of a certain age, with gray hair peeking out around the edges of his beret and a tightly trimmed beard, began looking for a suitable background. Light meters, cameras, tripods and vigorous discussions filled the garden. After a trial of several locations, it was finally agreed that the group should have the Pic St. Loup behind them. It was 3:10 when Fitch and Homer spotted a speck in the sky coming silently toward the mazet. Fitch and Homer, who were watching from the unicorn's back, could barely contain themselves. The beautiful colorful balloon got closer and closer as it drifted on a warm current of air.

Monsieur Seuffert Sr. had actually finished the photos of Grandma Biche and her grandchildren, but he kept posing everyone to delay the surprise as long as he could. Several cars were heard coming down the lane, and when Grandma Biche turned around to look after them, the huge blue and gold balloon was almost as low as the grapevines. She gasped with surprise, and Monsieur Seuffert Sr. snapped his last photo.

Eight or nine nieces, nephews and cousins piled out of the cars, and very quickly, the ropes were being pulled and the balloon landed at the edge of the lawn. It was the most awesome sight Homer and Fitch had ever seen. The operator, who introduced himself as Monsieur Beauquier, reached up and pulled on a short rope from time to time. When he did that, flames filled the opening at the bottom of the balloon, followed by a whooshing sound and then silence. Jean-Claude and La Biche explained to Grandma Biche that the balloon ride was part of her birthday gift and that other surprises were planned for the day. Jean-Claude had to give her his hanky for her glasses, and then there was a lot of hugging and kissing.

Grandma Biche, now aboard, waved good-bye to her family and friends as Monsieur Beauquier pulled the rope to let the flames fill the opening of the balloon. It slowly began to rise above the vineyards.

The hot-air balloon was beautiful. As they stared up at it, Homer told Fitch that it looked like a replica of one of the first hot-air balloons ever made, which he had seen in an encyclopedia. Even though this one had all the modern fittings, the pictures painted on it made it look like the one that had been first flown in 1783 by the Montgolfier brothers. Just like Monsieur Beauquier's, that one was blue with gold and red portraits on the sides and large ornate patterns.

"The Montgolfier brothers were French, you know. They sent a sheep, a rooster and a duck up to prove you could breathe." Homer giggled a little and so did Fitch.

Fitch looked at Homer in amazement. "Is there anything you don't know?" he asked. Homer's antennae drooped, and he looked as if he would disappear into his shell at any moment.

"Oh, no," said Fitch in a reassuring tone. "I didn't mean it like that! I just don't know how you know so many things and I don't seem to know much at all. I love having you as my best friend." And he gently stroked Homer's shell with one of his paws.

Homer's antennae perked up and he smiled. "Oh, Fitch," he began, "you know so much about the world and people, and everybody likes you. I've just spent a lot of my life reading books while you have had all the adventures. You are my best friend too, Fitch. I …" He hesitated then, so Fitch finished the sentence.

"I think that we are both very lucky to have found each other and that we each have different things that make us special." Homer smiled at that.

A sudden burst of activity turned their attention back to the balloon. It was coming back to earth! The cousins ran for the lines to hold it down. Fitch could see Grandma Biche waving, and the unicorn went closer to see what was needed. Before they knew what was happening, Fitch and Homer were in the gondola with Grandma Biche. She had invited them to come along!

Everyone cheered as the lines were released and the fire shot up into the huge opening at the bottom of the balloon. Fitch hugged

141

Grandma Biche, and both boys thanked her over and over.

"I asked Monsieur Beauquier if anyone else could join us, but he said we would be too heavy, and then I thought of you two. He agreed immediately," she said with a twinkle in her eye.

The balloon had gone up quite a bit by now, and as they looked down, they could see everyone below still waving and cheering. Fitch noticed that all the decorated tables were back in the yard and that Jean-Claude seemed to be testing the fairy lights again as they flickered just a bit.

The air was quite still, and everyone noticed how wonderfully silent it was. What a magnificent feeling to just be floating over the countryside! St. Mathieu de Treviers, the village closest to the mazet, was soon right under the balloon. Monsieur Beauquier opened a flap on the top of the balloon using another rope, and the balloon began to descend. As they got lower, Fitch thought he could hear cheering and shouting from the ground. He held on tightly and leaned over the edge to see what was causing all the noise.

The village square was full of people! Grandma Biche leaned over the edge too just as a large banner was unrolled to reveal the words JOYEUX ANNIVERSAIRE, VIVE LA MUSIQUE! Homer's little

143

antennae were waving wildly as he translated for Fitch, "Happy Birthday, Long Live Our Music!" Suddenly, the air was filled with music. Monsieur Beauquier lowered the balloon even more as several rows of children began to play wonderful flute music. Grandma Biche waved and waved as villagers followed the balloon through the town and out into the fields.

The Pic St. Loup was very close now, and the balloon rose higher so they could have a better view of the countryside. But soon Monsieur Beauquier opened the top flap and the balloon began to descend toward Le Triadou, another tiny village tucked in among the vineyards. Again a cheer went up from a group gathered in the center of the little village. Christmas lights were strung up on the trees, which created a very inviting mood. Everyone in the village had brought their cars to the town square, and just as Monsieur Beauquier began to open the burner to lift the gondola up, everyone beeped their horns and flashed their headlights. Grandma Biche waved and waved. Village after village made a celebration for Grandma Biche. Music, banners, cheering, waving and singing greeted her time and time again.

The balloon had caught a wonderful air current, and the ride was smooth and comfortable. The rows of grapevines looked lush and green from the sky, and the harvesters waved their hats as the company passed overhead. Near Ste. Croix de Quintillargue, Fitch spotted a large flock of sheep. Monsieur Beauquier took them down for a closer look. Several of the shepherds waved, and Fitch spotted Monsieur Richard, who had come past the mazet with his flock. It was amazing to see how many sheep there really were! Everyone waved and shouted greetings.

Suddenly, Monsieur Beauquier jerked the burner rope as hard as he could. The balloon silently began to lift up, and Fitch could see by his face that Monsieur Beauquier was very worried. At that moment, the steeple of the church in Valflaunès passed by the side of the gondola. It was only inches away! Grandma Biche's eyes got huge, and Homer, who had been on Fitch's shoulder, rolled into the pocket of Fitch's shirt. A fine line of perspiration appeared on Monsieur Beauquier's upper lip, which he quickly wiped off with his dark blue handkerchief.

"The wind always wants to play games," Homer translated Monsieur Beauquier's comments for Fitch.

145

It was late afternoon by the time the ropes were thrown over the edge and the gondola touched down behind the mazet.

Grandma Biche thanked Monsieur Beauquier many times for the wonderful ride, as did Fitch and Homer. Everyone waved and cheered as the burner whooshed and the flames shot up. The balloon rose quickly, and before long, Monsieur Beauquier was out of sight.

Grandma Biche began to cry with surprise and joy when she saw the transformation that had taken place in her garden. The fairy lights sparkled in every tree. Tables were heaped with wonderful food and gifts. Neighbors from miles around had come to celebrate. The party was spectacular. Just when everyone thought they couldn't eat another crumb, Uni and La Biche carried out a beautiful birthday cake.

"Oh, my!" gasped Homer to Fitch. "That's a *croque en bouche*."

"A what?" said Fitch.

"A *croque en bouche*—'crunch in your mouth,'" said Homer. "Those are tiny puff pastries filled with a delicious cream and then piled up like a pyramid. A special sugar syrup glaze is poured over them. The sugar glaze hardens so that when you bite it, it cracks in your mouth!"

The whole company sang "Happy Birthday" in French and then in English. By the time that was finished, everyone had been served a piece of dessert.

"Does it crunch in your mouth?" Homer asked Fitch as they began to eat. Fitch was enjoying it so much, he could only smile and nod. After dessert, a group of musicians—all family and friends—brought out musical instruments and set up the folding chairs in a half circle.

La Biche and Uni began preparing the next surprise. They carried the white butterfly boxes out into the garden, where they opened them up. The sky was immediately filled with butterflies of every color. The unicorn came back over to sit with Homer and Fitch to watch the show.

The musicians started to play. The butterflies arranged themselves in beautiful patterns and intricate designs to the music. The sunlight slowly slipping toward the horizon made an ideal backdrop for them, and the sparkle of the day's last rays accentuated their colors and patterns. Some of them would wait in the grass or on the trees, becoming invisible as they did, then they would suddenly soar up to form another picture. Everyone clapped and cheered, and even after their last performance—spelling out "Happy Birthday"—the audience called them back for two more encores. The movements of the butterflies perfectly accompanied the music, and once the wondrous show was over, the musicians all took bows to still more applause and cheers.

It was time for the gifts to be opened. What an array of wonderful things! Wrapping paper, ribbons and bows were piled all around by the time Grandma Biche was finished. When it seemed that all of the presents had been opened, Monsieur St. Bauzille stepped forward with a large box wrapped in silver paper and tied with a beautiful blue ribbon. He embraced Grandma Biche, whom he had known for many years.

"La Biche, Jean-Claude and your American friends commissioned this for you. I have made it with your lovely garden in mind, Emily," he said, bowing a little as he stepped back.

Grandma Biche began to open the box, and a hush fell over the guests. Everyone was holding their breath waiting to see what Monsieur St. Bauzille had created. The wrapping now off, Grandma

148

Biche held the beautiful glass bowl covered in colorful butterflies up for everyone to see. Oohs and aahs filled the quiet evening air. Grandma Biche hugged everyone, and Fitch noticed a few tears running down the side of her face.

The musicians began to play again, and some of the guests started to dance. Those who weren't dancing sat in small groups talking and laughing.

"Would you like to help me set up the fireworks?" Jean-Claude whispered to Fitch.

"That would be very exciting," thought Fitch. Homer had gone to talk to Monsieur St. Bauzille. So Fitch hopped on Jean-Claude's back, and off they went to the meadow behind the mazet.

"No one knows about this surprise," he said in a quiet voice to Fitch.

Fitch was all grins; he loved being a part of surprises best of all.

Chapter 12
Another Reunion

Fitch rolled over slowly in his cheese box bed. He didn't open his eyes but just pulled the quilt up around his ears. The clock on Grandma Biche's mantel began to strike. *Bong, bong, bong, bong, bong, bong, bong, bong, bong.* "Nine o'clock," thought Fitch, who had nearly fallen back to sleep before the clock ceased striking. Eyes still shut, he stuck his nose out from under the quilt and sniffed. "No hot chocolate, no toast, no other good smells," he thought. It was very quiet in the mazet. "It must be too early to get up." And he drifted off again.

It was well past 11:30 before anyone got up that morning. Grandma Biche said she had never slept that late in her life. She hugged La Biche's shoulders as her granddaughter sat eating brunch. One by one, everyone eventually made their way to the kitchen table.

The birthday party had been such fun that none of the guests had left until the moon was starting to fade from the sky. Friends from the surrounding villages came late into the evening. The night had been very warm for September, and Fitch thought that the fireworks, which he and Jean-Claude had set off, might have attracted some additional guests. No one had come empty-handed either. Gift boxes and platters of food were piled everywhere. The first rays of pink were peeking through the trees by the time Fitch had finally dropped onto his quilt. It had been the most wonderful party anyone could ever have imagined.

Everyone was still at the table talking about the party when Jean-Claude arrived. Grandma Biche poured him a large steaming cup of café au lait.

"I hate to be the bearer of bad news," he began, "but I have to leave for Paris tomorrow on business for my company." The mazet got very silent. Homer stopped chewing on his endive leaf and his antennae drooped. Fitch put his paw on Homer's shell, but he could feel a lump forming in his own throat.

There was a pause before Uni said, "We, too, must begin our departure plans, I'm sad to say. I know I speak for all of us when I say this was a most marvelous visit." She came closer to Fitch and Homer, who were looking very sad now. "I know you have made some wonderful friends," she told them, "but I also know we will all see one another again very soon."

Fitch was always surprised at how much better he felt after the unicorn explained things. And he had to admit that he missed Temenos Inn and his family just a little bit more than he had expected to. He looked at Homer, who sniffled a little but managed a smile. Grandma Biche came over by them. She patted Homer's shell and hugged Fitch. Then she leaned down and said almost in a whisper, "You never know what tomorrow will bring."

"That's true," thought Fitch, "that's very, very true."

Nico's ears stood up, and he jumped to his feet and barked just as a horn beeped out at the gate. It was Monsieur Richard's small green van. Everyone went out to the gate to greet him.

"My wife, Theresa, wanted me to give you these knit slippers to thank you for your hospitality to the sheep." With that, he handed Grandma Biche a package wrapped in pale yellow paper.

Fitch couldn't help but be curious about the contents of the van. He asked La Biche to lift him up so he could peek in the window. There on the floor of the van, nestled in straw, were two of the tiniest lambs he had ever seen.

Grandma Biche opened her gift and marveled at the slippers. They were a perfect fit, she exclaimed, and she was delighted at how warm she would be in them in the wintertime. "The stone floor does get quite cold," she admitted.

"Of course, we couldn't forget our new friends," said Monsieur Richard as he took out another package and handed it to the unicorn. "Or our old friends," he added, handing two smaller white packages to La Biche and Jean-Claude.

Everyone was so surprised at the gifts that they just stared at the packages in their hands. *"Allez y,"* Monsieur Richard said after a moment or two. La Biche was soon unwrapping a lovely long blue and white scarf, and Jean-Claude's scarf matched, which La Biche thought made the homemade gifts even more special. Uni unwrapped a knit wool shawl with a long fringe on the edge. She put it over her shoulders and modeled it for everyone. Two small envelopes fell from the folds as she twirled around.

"Open those, too," said Monsieur Richard with a chuckle. One held a black beret for Fitch, and the other contained an afghan square for Homer to sleep on.

"His wife thought my flowerpot might be drafty in the winter," Homer translated for Fitch.

"Well, I have to go now," Monsieur Richard said as he started up his van. "Have a safe trip home. Now you have something to remind you to come back to France." He waved as his little van started off down the lane.

Everyone waved in return and called, *"Merci beaucoup, merci beaucoup"* as he drove away.

The unicorn went off to prepare the airplane. Homer and Grandma Biche returned inside to examine additional details Homer had noticed on their cave and fossil specimens. Later in the afternoon, when Fitch, La Biche and Jean-Claude got back from a long walk, they found magnifying glasses, textbooks, specimens and specimen boxes covering Grandma Biche's kitchen table. It had been a warm sunny day, and much to the walking party's surprise, they had been able to gather a basketful of the little gray mushrooms. Homer took one and inspected it under the magnifying lens.

Uni returned to the mazet shortly thereafter and reported that the airplane was ready to go. She suggested that an early departure the following morning would be best. Suitcases were packed and then

154

repacked in an attempt to accommodate all the wonderful things they each wanted to take home. In addition to all the mementos Fitch and Homer had collected, Grandma Biche had prepared a carton of her special pots of jam, and Madame Millifera, the lady who kept some of her bees in the boxes under the oaks in the garden, had left several pots of honey for them to take home too. It wasn't until Uni gave her assistance that things finally seemed to fit. Then Jean-Claude said that he thought everything would fit into Grandma Biche's car, including the rickshaw, and he offered to drive them to the airport in the morning.

This seemed like an excellent plan, so right after supper, everything was packed in the car trunk, dishes were quickly washed, and teeth were thoroughly brushed. Sitting around the fireplace, which crackled and sparked, everyone sang songs and told stories and recounted their favorite part of the trip. The company became quiet as the fire started to turn to glowing embers. Nico was already asleep on his rug when La Biche yawned and said she needed to go to bed. Grandma Biche got extra hugs and kisses from everyone before the last light was turned out. By the time the moon was up over the trees, everyone was asleep.

Grandma Biche rose the next morning before anyone else started to stir. Fitch, who had opened one eye, saw she was preparing a lovely brioche for the oven. He dozed off again until the smell of the fresh baked goods made his whiskers twitch.

The sun was just peeking over the horizon as Jean-Claude opened the shutters before breakfast. The delicious warm brioche with butter and blackberry jam disappeared quickly, and Grandma Biche gave Fitch a special slice of goat's milk cheese to finish off his meal.

"Good-byes are always a mixture of sadness and happiness," said Grandma Biche as she hugged Fitch and Homer one last time. She stood at the gate in her white apron, with Nico at her side, waving good-bye until they turned out of the lane and onto the main road.

Things at the airport went very smoothly. The unicorn's preparatory visit the day before along with Jean-Claude's assistance in loading their baggage made their departure a quick process. Fitch and Homer noticed La Biche wiping her eyes after she gave Jean-Claude one last hug.

Soon the unicorn opened the cockpit window and called, "Clear." The engine came to life, and in moments, they had left the runway and had begun to climb. The unicorn turned the plane back toward the airport and made a low pass, tipping the plane's wing to Jean-Claude. He waved until they were out of sight. A moment later, they were over the mazet. The unicorn circled over the vineyards, and when she tipped the wings, first to the left and then to the right, they could see Grandma Biche waving to them from the orchard. Even Homer didn't cry because he knew they would be back.

The airplane rose higher and higher. The patchwork quilt of land below was soon hidden in a blanket of white clouds. Everyone was quiet. During the trip, Fitch passed out sandwiches and cold drinks from the coolers, but most of the time, he just pulled his new beret over his eyes and dozed. Homer read for a while from a large leather-bound book Grandma Biche had given him, but he, too, spent most of the trip asleep.

"November 8336 Mike requests landing instructions," Uni was saying when Fitch finally woke up and realized they were home. He gently roused Homer and held him up to the window to watch the trees get larger and larger as they approached the ground. Then the runway came into view in front of them. With a little bump, the wheels hit the ground. The airplane rolled to the taxi lane, turned and then stopped on the tarmac in front of the hangar. They were home!

What no one had anticipated was the welcome party that now poured out of the airport office. What a reunion! Fitch's grandfather had brought Homer's family and all of Fitch's family including Grandmother Mouse on his motorcycle, which now had a sidecar.

Introductions were quickly made. Alvin, Homer's little brother, was even shyer than Homer. Alvin hugged his big brother's shell and didn't want to let go even long enough for Homer to unpack the gifts he had brought back. Freddy and Sally crowded around Fitch too. But Teddy, after giving his younger brother a hug, had gone to inspect the airplane. Fitch's parents were very happy to see their son, and lots of wonderful stories were exchanged while everyone snacked on the last of the food in the coolers.

Homer signaled to Fitch that he needed a private word. "What is it, Homer?" Fitch asked as they stepped away from the group. Homer seemed to be very distressed.

"Well," he began, "it's my little brother," and he put his head down. A large tear escaped and ran down his face. "He wants me to come home, and … well, I want to go, but I don't want to leave you and Uni." Another tear leaked down his face. He sniffed a little.

"You won't be leaving us," Fitch said in a comforting tone as he pulled out his T-shirt so Homer could wipe his eyes. "Not at all. It will be like … like …" He paused. "It'll be like Jean Claude," he said with sudden inspiration. "Like Jean-Claude, you'll go on a little business trip. You'll come back to Temenos Inn when you finish your 'home business'!"

"What a great idea," said Uni, who had come up quietly behind them.

"Yes," said Homer, "that makes it all feel better in my heart."

Fitch patted Homer's shell. "We've been through a lot, buddy," he said.

"No one ever called me buddy before," Homer said as he managed a little smile.

And that's how it all got worked out. Grandfather Mouse would bring Homer back to Temenos Inn after he finished his "home business." But right now everyone gave lots of hugs and kisses. Fitch showed Sally, Teddy and Freddy how the French give three kisses on the cheeks. Sally loved doing it, but Teddy and Freddy weren't too sure.

Homer, his parents and Alvin, still clinging to Homer, were settled in the motorcycle's sidecar. Fitch's family got in next. There was lots of room for everyone and all the gifts, too. Grandfather Mouse revved the motor, winked at Fitch, and off they went.

Fitch, Uni and La Biche then unpacked the rest of the plane and reassembled the rickshaw. When all was in order, they set off toward home. Fall had come to the area while they had been gone. The trees were red and yellow, and the forest behind La Biche's cottage was as lovely as her butterflies.

"Thank you, Uni," she said as she helped her friend back into the harness of the rickshaw after they dropped off the deer. "I had a wonderful time, and I can never thank you enough."

But Uni wouldn't let her say any more. "We loved your family, La Biche, and I'm sure we had as much fun as you did." The unicorn touched La Biche gently on her head with her horn. La Biche smiled and waved as Fitch and Uni pulled away toward Temenos Inn.

A few minutes later, Fitch watched as a field of flowers and tall grass faded away to be replaced by a beautiful trellis with roses, a brick path, a garden and at last Temenos Inn.

They unpacked quickly. The rickshaw was wiped down and stored in the toolshed. It had started to get dark very early now, as the year would soon be drawing to a close. After an early supper, the unicorn built a fire in the fireplace because the evening was surprisingly chilly. "I'm glad Homer has his woolly square to keep out the damp," said Uni as she pulled her new French shawl over her shoulders. Fitch smiled. He was in his new red flannel cowboy pajamas with matching tail warmer, a little gift his mother had given him at the airport.

They snuggled up together in Uni's big rocking chair in front of the fire, with Fitch in his usual place on the large armrest. Slowly rocking back and forth, they talked about their wonderful trip until Fitch started getting very tired. The fire was dying down. "Yes, it was

quite an adventure," said Uni after a long silence.

Half asleep and with his eyes already closed, Fitch remembered Grandma Biche's words. "You never know what tomorrow will bring," he said in a sleepy voice.

162

Strangely enough, just at that moment, a mysterious letter with interesting stamps addressed to Fitch at Temenos Inn was being dropped in a mailbox. …

About the Author

Sheila Brogan was born and grew up on a farm in Wisconsin, not too far from the Temenos Inn. She has been telling stories for many years, but this is the first time she has written one down. An old grade school report card mentioned that while her spelling was a problem, Sheila was a good writer and should compose more. Sometimes it takes a while for one to accept good advice. She has lived in Canada, Illinois, Florida and Long Island, New York. She and her family currently live in New Jersey, where she works as a nurse.

For more information about Fitch go to his web site at :

WWW.adventuresoffitch.com

Printed in the United States
64915LVS00003B/160-168